"A HEARTRENDING TALE BOTH WISE AND WORTHY . . .

Berg keeps a tight grip on readers as she takes us back and forth from a 12-year-old's perspective to the memories and secrets revealed at the reunion—35 years later—of three sophisticated, mature women. By its finish, the story has taken your breath away with its twists and turns; it delivers an impact that stays with you well past the ending."
—*Rocky Mountain News*

"In her earlier novel, *Talk Before Sleep*, Berg was able to draw together remarkable humor and incredible pain with enormous insight into their intricate relationship. She does so again in *What We Keep*."
—*The Seattle Times*

"Fans of Elizabeth Berg are familiar with her extraordinary talent for description—you can almost taste, feel, and hear her novels with amazing intensity. . . . The poignant twists of rejection and eventual redemption will pull you along at full throttle, making you happy you stayed for the tear-jerking, life-affirming finale."
—*Detroit Free Press*

"Elizabeth Berg remembers what it was like to be a child. . . . She gets it all delightfully right."
—*The Cleveland Plain Dealer*

Please turn the page for more reviews. . . .

"A BEAUTIFULLY WRITTEN STORY . . .
Berg has an almost painterly gift for choosing the telling detail. She neatly accomplishes that most ephemeral trick of memory."
—*St. Louis Post-Dispatch*

"Berg is very good, as always, at reconstructing the emotional and conversational rhythms of girls on the edge of adolescence."
—*New York Daily News*

"Compelling . . . *What We Keep* takes the reader back to a time when TV didn't occupy every waking moment, when Mom was generally at home, and when families ate there together. A big night out might be a trip to Dairy Queen."
—*San Antonio Express-News*

What We Keep "bring[s] to mind such highbrow novels of girlhood as Lisa Shea's *Hula* and Susan Minot's *Monkeys*. . . . Ginny's shame, anger, guilt, and sorrow are presented with subtlety and suave humor in Berg's novel, which manages to be charming and painful at the same time."
—*The Baltimore Sun*

Also by Elizabeth Berg

WHAT WE KEEP

A NOVEL

Elizabeth Berg

BALLANTINE BOOKS • NEW YORK

A Ballantine Book
Published by The Random House Publishing Group

Copyright © 1998 by Elizabeth Berg

Published in the United States by Ballantine Books, an imprint of The Random House Publishing Group, a division of Random House, Inc., New York, and simultaneously in Canada by Random House of Canada Limited, Toronto.

Ballantine and colophon are registered trademarks of Random House, Inc.

www.ballantinebooks.com

ISBN 0-345-43502-8

This edition published by arrangement with Random House, Inc.

Manufactured in the United States of America

First Ballantine Books Trade Paperback Edition: June 1999
First Ballantine Books Mass Market Edition: January 2002

OPM   9   8   7   6   5

To women who risk telling the hard truths

ACKNOWLEDGMENTS

*Thanks to my editor, Kate Medina,
and to my agent, Lisa Bankoff.
Always true.*

China
Decorates our table
Funny how the cracks don't
Seem to show

You're right next to me
But I need an airplane
I can feel the distance
Getting close

—From "China," by Tori Amos

Outside the airplane window the clouds are thick and rippled, unbroken as acres of land. They are suffused with peach-colored, early morning sun, gilded at the edges. Across the aisle, a man is taking a picture of them. Even the pilot couldn't keep still—"Folks," he just said, "we've got quite a sunrise out there. Might want to have a look." I like it when pilots make such comments. It lets me know they're awake.

Whenever I see a sight like these clouds, I think maybe everyone is wrong; maybe you *can* walk on air. Maybe we should just try. Everything could have changed without our noticing. Laws of physics, I mean. Why not? I want it to be true that such miracles occur. I want to stop the plane, put the kickstand down, and have us all file out there, shrugging airline claustrophobia off our shoulders. I want us to be able to breathe easily this high up, to walk on clouds as if we were angels, to point out our houses to each other way, way, way down there; and there; and there. How proud we would suddenly feel about where we live, how tender toward everything that's ours—our Mixmasters, resting on kitchen counters; our children, wearing the socks we bought them and going about children's business; our mail lying on our desks; our gardens, tilled and expectant. It seems to

1

me it would just come with the perspective, this rich
appreciation.

I lean my forehead against the glass, sigh. I am forty-
seven years old and these longings come to me with the
same seriousness and frequency that they did when I was
a child.

"Long trip, huh?" the woman next to me asks.

"Oh," I say. "Yes. Although . . . Well, I sighed because
I wish I could get out. You know? Get out there and walk
around."

She looks past me, through the window. "Pretty," she
says. And then, "Of course, you'd die."

"Oh, well. What's not dangerous?"

"Beats me," the woman says. "Not food. Not water.
Not air, not sex. You can't do *anything*. Well, maybe put
your name on the list for Biosphere." We smile, ruefully.
She's pretty, a young blond businesswoman wearing a
stylish navy-blue suit, gold jewelry, soft-looking leather
heels now slipped off her feet. At first, she busied herself
with paperwork. Now she's bored and wants to talk.
Fine with me. I'm bored, too.

"Do you ever think that this is the end of the world?" I
ask. "I mean, don't get me wrong—"

"Oh, I know what you mean," she says. "I do think
about that. Dying planets, how . . . unspecial we are, really.
Just the most current thing in the line since paramecia."

The flight attendant stops her cart beside us, asks if
we'd like a drink. This seems petty, considering the con-
tent of our conversation. Still, I request orange juice; the
woman beside me says she'd like a scotch.

"You know what?" I tell the flight attendant. "I think
I'll have a scotch, too." I have always wondered who in

the world would want a cocktail on an early morning flight. Now I know: people with a load on their minds that they would like very much to lighten.

After my seatmate and I have pulled down our trays and set up our impromptu bar, I say, "I don't even like scotch."

"Me neither." She shrugs, takes a sip, grimaces. "But I really hate flying. Sometimes this helps."

I smile, extend my hand. "I'm Ginny Young."

"Martha Hamilton."

"You live in California?"

"Yeah. San Francisco. You?"

"I live in Boston. I'm going to visit my mother. She lives in Mill Valley."

"Nice. How long since you've seen her?"

I do some math, then answer, "Thirty-five years."

Martha turns toward me, stares. I know her scotch is pooled in her mouth.

I shrug. "I don't like my mother. I'm not ashamed to say that. She's not a good person. She did some things . . . Well, she's not a good person." Whenever people I've met tell their mother horror stories, I save mine for last. It's the best, because it's the worst.

"So . . . why are you going to see her?"

"It was my sister's idea. She thinks she's sick. Not my mother—her."

"Is she?"

"Don't know. She's waiting for some test results. But she wanted to go and see our mother. Just . . . in case. You know. Unfinished business that she feels she needs to attend to."

Martha breathes out. "Jesus. I'm sorry."

"Well."

She touches my arm. "Are you all right?"

"Me? Yes! It's . . . this is old. It's so old. I didn't intend ever to see my mother again, and I was perfectly comfortable with that. I won't see her after this visit; I know that. I'm just doing this for my sister. Even though I don't really think she's sick. She can't be."

Martha nods, cracks an ice cube with her teeth, then looks at me, one eyebrow raised.

"Right," I say. "I know."

"I'll tell you something," Martha says. "I was in a cemetery last week, walking my dog. You're not supposed to walk your dog there, so when I heard someone coming, I hid behind this big marker. I saw a woman stop just a few graves away. She knelt down and started talking out loud. She was apparently talking about one of her kids who was giving her a really hard time, and then she said, 'I didn't do that to you, Ma, did I? Did I?' And then she lay down and just started crying. She cried so *hard*! It was one of those things where the grief is so raw, you can't help yourself—you start crying, too. And when I started crying, my dog started barking. The woman looked up and saw me, of course. She got all embarrassed—jumped up and wiped her face, started straightening her clothes and rummaging around in her purse for something or other. And I felt terrible. It was terrible to have a dog there, those rules are absolutely right. I apologized, but I still felt like a jerk.

"All the way home, I wondered what that woman was crying about, what she had remembered. I wondered if other daughters talk to their mothers when they visit their graves, whether if, when my mother dies, I will.

Seems like a good party question, doesn't it?—What would you say at your mother's grave? Well, maybe not a *party* question. But an interesting one. At least you'll have the chance to speak to her in person."

"Right," I say, although what I'm thinking is, there's nothing I want to tell my mother. I'm only going for Sharla. I love my sister; I'm finished with my mother, have been for a long time. Not for nothing did I sit in therapists' offices going through a forest's worth of Kleenex.

"Where does your sister live?" Martha asks.

"Texas. San Antonio. She'll be at the airport waiting; her flight gets in twenty minutes before mine."

"Has *she* seen your mother in all this time?"

"No."

"Wow. This will be some meeting."

"I know," I say, and drain what's left of the scotch. Then I squeeze the plastic glass to see how far I can bend it. Not far: it cracks in my hand. I put it in the throw-up bag, fold the top over, place it neatly in the center of my tray table. I don't want to talk anymore. I lean back, look out the window. I have my reasons, I tell myself—and Martha, too, in case she's picking up on my thoughts—she's from California, after all; they do stuff like that. But I do have my reasons. I absolutely do.

"Miss?" the flight attendant asks. "Breakfast?" I startle, then smile and nod yes to the fat slices of French toast she is offering me. I am probably the only one in the world who likes airline food. I appreciate the inventive garnishes, the only-for-you serving sizes. I like the taste of the salad dressings. When the entrée is something like pizza, I think, well, isn't that the cutest thing. Naturally, I don't admit this to anyone.

Martha has opted for the cheese omelet, and when I watch her cut it neatly in half, I wish I'd gotten one, too. She shrugs after her first bite, the physical equivalent of "Yuck." I smile, shrug back, pour the thick artificial maple syrup over my French toast. It looks delicious.

"I saw a row of three across open back there," Martha says, after she's eaten most of her breakfast. "I think I'll go on back and stretch out for a while."

"Okay."

"Unless you were thinking of that, too. In that case, we could flip for it."

"No, this is fine," I say. "I'll have more room, too. Anyway, I'm not going to sleep."

"Really? Any plane trip over an hour, I have to sleep. Otherwise I get stir-crazy. Once I brought letters to read on an airplane. You know, the kind of thing you keep, thinking sometime you'd really like to read them again, but then you never do. I brought along this huge stack of letters from old boyfriends. I took them out and read them all. They passed the time all right, but it was so embarrassing—they made me cry. I'll never do that again! Better to go to sleep and embarrass yourself by drooling." She stands, opens the overhead bin and pulls down a pillow and a blanket, heads down the aisle.

I know what Martha means about old letters. One rainy day after my younger daughter had gone to school, I went down into the basement and got out my battered cardboard box of love letters. I brought it up to the bedroom and dumped it out on the bed. Then I remember putting on this old purple cardigan that had a rip at the elbow—it was a little cold—and I sat and read those letters. All of them: sweet, morning-after notes full of misspellings that Tom Winchell had taped onto my bathroom mirror; fountain-penned missives from Tim Stanley, who went on to study theology, and I know why—so he could stand in a pulpit and talk, talk, talk. I read things that made me get soft at the center again, that made me stare out the window and sigh. I got absolutely lost in reverie; I felt really out of it for hours after I'd finished reading those letters. I almost called one of my old boyfriends, but I could anticipate what would happen. I would pour out a rush of sentiment—"Now, this doesn't mean anything, but do you remember, do you remember the incredible *love* we felt for each other, do you remember when we stayed out all night to watch the sun come up by the river and you put your jacket around me and I had a cut on my lip and you kissed me so gently it made me think I could never, never leave you?" I'd say something like that and the now-balding Larry Drever, holding the phone at the desk from which he sells life insurance, would say, ". . . *Who* is this?"

So I know it's dangerous to reenter the past. Especially when things come back to you as strongly as they do to me. I'm extremely good at remembering, have had this ability since I was very young. Give me one rich detail, and I'll reconstruct a whole scene. Say "Dairy Queen," and I'll recall a night in high school when I was there with a bunch of friends and a cloud of gnats hung around Joe Antillo's head and he reached up to swat them away and spilled his root-beer float all over himself and Trudy Jameson, who was wearing a blue shirt tied at the waist, and jeans with one back pocket torn off and her silver charm bracelet and "Intimate" perfume. She had a cold that night. A few days earlier, her eight-year-old brother Kevin had fallen off his bicycle and cut his knee so badly he'd required seven stitches, half of which he removed later that night with his sister's manicure scissors—"just to see what would happen," he told his horrified parents when they drove him back to the emergency room. "How do you remember all these details?" people ask me all the time. I don't know how. I just do. One image leads to another, then another, as though they're all strung together. And in any given memory I summon up, I become again the person I was then—I feel the weather, I feel everything. I lose the person I am now to some other, younger self.

It can hurt you, remembering—the shock of reentry, the mild disorientation, the inevitable sadness that accompanies a true vision of the past. Still, right now, staring out the window at the land far below me, realizing I have no idea where I am, I want nothing more than to do absolutely that. I want to go back to the time when I started to lose my mother, and search for clues as to why and how. I suppose it's about time. I lean my seat back. Close my eyes. Begin.

*I*t started in 1958, in the very small town of Clear Falls, Wisconsin, where I grew up. It was the summer I turned twelve, the year my thirteen-year-old sister Sharla and I began sneaking out of the house at night to sleep on the lawn. It was so hot and humid that year; we felt we couldn't breathe. The sheets were as irritating as army blankets against our bare limbs, and the tired fan in our bedroom only made things worse, blowing stale, warm air on us that my sister said felt like Uncle Roy trying to kiss us. This my mother's massively overweight brother did ceaselessly every Thanksgiving when he visited from Raleigh, though only in front of other people, so we felt less threatened than enraged. "Aren't y'all my girlfriends?" he would bellow, and we would say no, we were not. "Sure you are!" he'd say, and we would roll our eyes and be as rude as the proximity to our parents would allow.

We suspected our parents would object to our sleeping outside, so we never asked them if we could. Instead, we would wait until the grandfather clock downstairs bonged midnight in its old, metallic voice, and then we would tiptoe out—silent, we were sure, as any Indian ever was. We admired Indians. We dyed sheets with coffee and made long-stitched dresses out of them, cut the bottoms into unlikely looking fringes, and then cinched the

9

waists with beaded belts. We tucked our parakeet Lucky's discarded feathers into our hair and put on the moccasins we'd begged for at Christmas, even though their color was an untrue pink. We arranged rocks into circles for a campfire, hunted for squirrels and chipmunks in order to commune with animal spirits, and rolled jewel-colored berries in leaves for dinner.

Mostly, though, we practiced walking noiselessly through the woods behind our house. It wasn't easy. I thought the best approach was to *think* yourself very light, and to intuit where the twigs were—if you tried to see them all, you'd only fail.

Our parents went to bed early, as did virtually everyone in our neighborhood. No doubt we would have been safe exiting the house around ten, but midnight had a romantic and dangerous flair to it. Besides, we liked being on the cusp of something, being exactly between days, moving about like ghosts when Monday gave way to Tuesday. We thought if ever there was a time for the extraordinary to occur, this was it. And we longed for the extraordinary. People rooted in security often do.

All along one side of the house were lush white lilac bushes, and it was in them that we hid our sleeping blanket, an old quilt that our family once used for picnics—long after it had been used for many beds. The colors in the quilt—pinks, purples, yellows, greens—were faded beyond pastel; they resembled the bleeding edge of a watercolor, and the fabric was so worn it felt almost like touching nothing. The pattern was of flowers in a basket, and the person who made the quilt had embroidered a bee hovering over one of the roses. I liked thinking about how, a hundred years ago, someone else had been charmed by the sight of a bee and a flower, had believed it worth commenting on in this quiet way. I loved the natural world, too. I loved all aspects of science, in fact—everything I read having to do with that most elegant of subjects thrilled me, though usually I did not understand what I read. It was an oddity about me that the subject I had the most difficulty with was the one I loved most. I would stare at formulas and admire them for their spare beauty without being able to grasp their meaning. The fact that they cleanly explained some higher law to someone else was enough for me. It comforted me.

Sharla and I would spread the quilt out in the middle of the backyard and then stretch out luxuriously. We would spend some time contemplating the constellations, reciting to each other all the star lore we'd learned thus far. It seemed like an Indian thing to do. Plus it required the beautiful necessity of focusing on the dark heavens, letting the phase of the moon register on the back of the working eye. The grass was a deep blue color in the dim light of night; the smell was rich and horsey. The whine of the occasional mosquito was thrilling because we couldn't see the insect, and therefore our minds made it roughly the size of a little airplane. We wore sleeveless T-shirts and waist-high underwear, the white cotton uniform of the flat-chested.

Just before dawn, when the sky lit up at the bottom with its hopeful shade of gray/pink, we would sneak back into the house. Now our beds were acceptable, and we would pull down the shades and sleep until around ten, then come tousle-headed and blinking into the kitchen for a breakfast of peanut-butter toast and orange juice. Except for those rare times when our mother wasn't home—when she put on her gloves and hat and took the bus to the dentist's, say. At those times, we would have miniature Coke floats, served in the thin, light-refracting champagne flutes our parents kept in the high cupboard over the refrigerator.

We had some thoughts about life that summer: it was a smooth and plodding thing, as comfortable as slippers. It was pleasantly predictable, widely safe. Without knowing exactly what our futures would hold, we nonetheless felt sure about the way to march toward them. Right was right. Wrong was wrong. The difference between the two was easy to see.

And then Jasmine Johnson moved in next door and set off reverberations in our minds and in our centers that would shape us more surely than anything else ever had, or would.

I was the one to see the moving van first. I came down-stairs early one Tuesday, bent on finding a "dew nest." This, according to my sister, was the morning home of the sacred Egyptian jewel spider, a delicate creature with a multicolored pattern on its back. Much prettier than your average spider. And capable of granting wishes. If you were so fortunate as to find one still in the nest, you put your hand over it, made a wish, kissed your fingertips, and, voilà, at the end of the day anything you desired would be yours. Anything. I half knew this was another one of my sister's fanciful lies—she believed in benign forms of torture—but I got up early just to check. My mother was in the kitchen making breakfast, the radio turned on low to "keep her company." Perry Como was singing one of his nice-guy songs and my mother hummed along shyly. She had a crush on Perry Como. She said that. It was all right; my father had a crush on Dinah Shore.

My mother was dressed in her beautiful yellow summer robe, the tie cinched evenly into a bow at the exact center of her waist, but her auburn hair was sticking up in the back, an occasional occurrence that I always hated seeing, since in my mind it suggested a kind of incompetence. It was an unruly cowlick, nearly impossible to

13

tame—I knew this, having an identical cowlick of my own—but I did not forgive its presence on my mother. It did not go with the rest of her looks: her deep blue eyes, her thin, sculptured nose, her high cheekbones, her white, white skin—all signs, I was certain, of some distant link with royalty. She would not pursue the notion; I intended to do it for her when I grew up. "There!" I would say one day, presenting her with papers embossed with gold seals. "Oh, my," she would say softly, handling the papers with a combination of wild joy and great delicacy. "Thank you, Ginny! I'm so sorry I didn't believe you. Thank you!"

"It's all right," I would say, wiping the tears from her old face. "At least you got to finally know."

As for now, my mother looked up from the electric frying pan to ask, "Where are *you* off to?"

"Your hair's sticking up," I answered.

"I know," she said, though she had not known. If she had, she would have fixed it. She put her hand to her head, pressed down, and I saw a hint of embarrassment, a rising up of pink to her cheeks. This was a tender thing; and I thought about crossing the room to hug her around the waist, to feel her hand with her loose wedding ring on the back of my head, cradling it, but I was getting older. And I had work to do. The spider had to be found still in the nest in order for its magic to work.

"I'm going out to look for something," I said. "I'll be right back."

"Do you want eggs?" my mother called after me. "Bacon?"

"No," I told her. "I'm going back to bed." Although as I stepped outside I realized I wasn't tired anymore. Early mornings invigorated me; it was the clean-slate aspect of them, the way the air seemed washed and expectant.

The screen door banged behind me. I stretched, searched the backyard, found nothing. Then, though I doubted the spider would be so public, I went into the front yard, and there it was, an orange monstrosity of a truck, backed up *over the lawn* to the front door of the house beside ours.

Mrs. O'Donnell lived next to us, and I had supposed she always would. She was a widow of indeterminate age. She was slow-gaited, but not dependent on a cane; she dressed in clothes that were dowdy but not quite grandmotherly; and she had a voice that was thin but not quivery. She wore thick bifocals with pale-blue frames, one side repaired—apparently permanently—with a tiny gold safety pin. Every spring she gave herself home permanents that were an advertisement against them: her steely gray hair reminded me of Brillo pads, minus the thrill of the hidden soap. She wore a dark-pink lipstick that disappeared from the middle of her mouth and caked at the edges of it, and excessive amounts of rouge that on anyone else my mother would call suggestive. With the exception of our annual Christmas cookie exchange and the halfhearted ritual of waving when we saw each other coming and going, she mostly kept to herself. I never saw anyone come to her house, except for her nephew Leroy, who was a cop. He would visit irregularly in his show-off work car, pull up in front of her house at an angle that suggested extreme emergency. He exited his vehicle with difficulty; his belly got in the way of the steering wheel. Sometimes when he left the house he would be carrying a brown paper bag folded over neatly at the top. I had no idea what was in there, but I liked to think that it was fried chicken, wrapped up in aluminum foil. A leg and a breast, which Leroy would eat while he sat in his car, waiting for speeders, longing for salt.

Last summer, for a few fever-pitched weeks, I had entered into the business of making and selling pot holders. Mrs. O'Donnell was my first customer. She bought a couple of the rose-and-green ones—my favorite, as well—and then invited me in for Rice Krispies treats. After she'd given me an impromptu tour of her house, we sat down together at the kitchen table. Then we both seemed to realize we had nothing whatsoever to say. I noticed faint brown stains on her tablecloth, next to an embroidered picture of three gray kittens in a basket, whose blue eyes seemed sad to me, lost and pleading.

"Oh, well," Mrs. O'Donnell finally said softly, looking up from her lap. I saw that her eyes were moist and that she had what appeared to be a bit of an infection in one of them.

I didn't want the treat anymore. Pinkeye had broken out spectacularly last spring in my elementary school. I was one of the few spared, and I didn't want to take any chances now. I looked around in a way I hoped didn't seem desperate, and finally commented on a rooster clock hanging on the kitchen wall. It was a black rooster, tail feathers drooping forlornly, comb and wattle faded to a dusty pink. The round face of a clock was trapped forever in his center—he would never seduce hens, or exuberantly salute the morning. Though I knew full well he was plastic and never stood a chance for such things, I nonetheless regretted for him this awful loss. The clock said 1:47, though the time was around ten-thirty.

"That's really nice," I said, smiling and nodding at the rooster.

"What is?"

I pointed behind her, and when she turned to look, I slipped the Rice Krispies treat into my shirt pocket.

"Would you like that clock?" Mrs. O'Donnell asked.

"Oh!" I said. "No, thank you; you keep it, I couldn't take that."

"To tell the truth, I'd forgotten I even had it. You're welcome to it."

"Oh," I said. And then, after a pause, "Uh-huh." Finally, "Thank you, that's very nice of you, but really . . ." I so very much did not want that clock. I knew it would be sticky with old grease, that there would be nothing at all I could do with it, not even take it apart to have a look at its innards. I was very interested that summer in taking things apart. I cracked open rocks with my father's hammer, rubbed gently the damp surfaces I found inside various pods I pulled from trees, ripped apart buds for the tight sight of embryonic flowers. I used a pearl-handled steak knife to saw open the high heels of a pair of party shoes my mother was throwing out, and on one brave day when no one else was home, unscrewed the back of the kitchen radio. I enjoyed several minutes of silent appreciation for the glowing tubes and copper wires I found there, adjusted the volume up and down ceaselessly, trying to see what *did* that.

Now I stared at the rooster clock, trying to imagine if there could be any single thing of value or interest to me in it. I had heard that there were jewels inside watches, but I didn't think anything like that lay inside that rooster; knew if I opened it I would notice nothing but perhaps a rising up of fine dust. I wanted to say clearly to Mrs. O'Donnell that I did not want the clock, but I wanted even more not to hurt her feelings. Therefore I remained silent, while long seconds passed. My stomach felt as though it were being wrung out; I curled and uncurled my toes slowly against the soles of my new flip-flops.

Finally, Mrs. O'Donnell smiled, closemouthed and vaguely regretful; I did the same. She nodded; I hesitated, then nodded, too. Then she said, "You know, you can take as many treats as you want, dear. But let me wrap them up for you. They'll stain your shirt if you keep them in your pocket that way."

Apart from that one visit, I never really talked to Mrs. O'Donnell. I didn't particularly regret her moving. I understood that this meant anything could happen; a kid my age might move in, for example. She might be an only child and I could become her best friend and profit by the spoiling she got from her parents. And we needed younger kids on the block; Sharla and I were the only ones under sixteen. I enjoyed very much the sight of teenage goodnight kissing that went on, both in cars pulled up in front of houses as well as the more chaste variety that took place under yellow porch lights; I thrilled to the screeching sound of peel-outs performed by the neighborhood boys whenever their parents were away; I noted with interest and envy the outfits worn by girlfriends walking down the sidewalks together: neat upside-down V-cuts in pedal pushers, blouses with the collar turned up, white leather bucket purses slung over shoulders, rabbits' feet on a chain at the side. Those girls wore fat lines of eyeliner, Fire-and-Ice lipstick.

I also liked seeing the teens come back from town with bags from the record store holding the latest 45s; liked knowing they'd probably also been to the drugstore for vanilla Cokes and fries, after which they might have gone behind the store to sneak a smoke. But I would have traded all that happily for some kids our age. If ever we'd taken the risk of telling hard truths, Sharla and I might have admitted to each other that we were lonely.

After I spied the moving van, I ran back in the house and told my mother Mrs. O'Donnell was moving.

"Is it today?" my mother asked. She went to the window, looked out at the van.

"Oh, it is. Poor thing." She returned to the stove, turned the bacon, drained some grease into an empty milk carton.

"How come you didn't say anything?" I asked. "How come you didn't tell me?"

"Well, I did. I'm sure I did."

"Nuh-uh," I said, which was my favorite expression. It was rakish, I thought. I recalled now, though, that my mother *had* told me. But it had been on a rainy day and I'd been reading, and I was close to the end of a chapter in a Nancy Drew book. Who could have expected me to hear anything when a pillow was being lowered onto Nancy's face?

"How come you called her 'poor thing'?" I asked.

"Oh. . . ." My mother laid the bacon out in neat rows on a paper towel.

"Can I have a piece, just one?" I now regretted saying

I didn't want breakfast; the smell of the bacon rivaled my mother's "My Sin."

"Yes, I made some for you."

Ah.

I took a piece of bacon, then sat at the kitchen table to eat it, one leg crossed over the other and swinging in order to maximize the flavor. "How come you said 'poor thing'?"

My mother cracked eggs into the frying pan, then bent and squinted at the dial, adjusting it. I liked when she did this. She looked like a scientist.

"Oh, you know," she said. She didn't want to tell me. Which meant that I must persist.

"*What?*"

"Well, she's old and all alone. Having some . . . problems. She's going to the nursing home."

"Oh." I didn't know much about nursing homes, except that the residents I'd seen there mostly sat like rag dolls in wheelchairs, staring. They were the recipients of many construction-paper projects that we did in school and then reluctantly delivered—May baskets, glittery valentines, turkeys made from handprints, Santas with cotton-ball beards. And you died there, I knew that. I had a flash of regret that I hadn't been kinder to Mrs. O'Donnell. It wouldn't have been so hard.

"Who's moving in?" I asked.

"I don't know—We'll see pretty soon, I guess. How many eggs do you want?"

"One," I said. "No. Two."

It was going to be a busy day; I wanted to be fortified. Everything Mrs. O'Donnell had in that house was about to be brought outside. Her ottoman and her scrapbooks.

All her pots and pans. Towels and rugs, the doilies she kept on her maple end tables. Her very bed. I would see everything she owned, carried by strong men in T-shirts up a ramp and into the dark mouth of the truck. When they left, the house would be empty. Not even a curtain. I shivered.

I hear someone rummaging around beside me and open my eyes to see Martha, digging in the seat pocket. "My reading glasses," she says. "I think I stuck them in here." She reaches in farther, pulls them out, and holds them up triumphantly.

"You decided not to sleep?" I say.

"I *did* sleep! It felt like such a long time, but it was only fifteen minutes. I had a dream and everything. I dreamed I had a baby—a little girl. Actually, from what I hear, that's a nightmare."

"What do you mean?"

"Oh, you know, how mean girls are to their mothers." Something inside me stiffens. "I don't think that's true."

"Do you have girls?"

"Two, ten and twelve."

"And they're nice to you?"

"Well, they have their moments. But all kids do."

"I don't know," Martha says. "I guess that incident in the cemetery reminded me of how hard girls can be on their mothers. I know I was—for the longest time, my mother just couldn't do anything right. It's like . . . Well, once I saw these two young women in an art museum, talking about a painting. One of them said, 'It's really

22

just the quality of differentness that I love so much here. I always want a little differentness in my art, don't you?' And the other woman said, 'Oh God, yes. I want everything in my life to be unusual. Except things like, you know, my *mother*.' And I thought, that's true. I wouldn't want my mother to be different, either. Yet I always despised her for being the same as everyone else." She looks at me. "Your kids aren't like that, thinking everything you do is wrong?"

"Not at all. We're very close."

"Huh," she says, and I have the feeling she doesn't believe me.

"We really are," I say. "I was close to my mother, too, until she screwed up so bad. And I was *very* close to my stepmother." I see her suddenly: Georgia, sitting at the side of my bed, taking down the hem of a dress I refused to part with and talking to me about a teacher who'd sent me to the principal. She wasn't mad at me; she was mad at the teacher. She had a call in to him.

"I wonder if your daughters will change when they get older," Martha says. "I hear when they hit the teen years, they can really—"

"They'll be fine," I say. "I waited a long time to have kids. My first was born at thirty-five. I wanted to be absolutely sure I was ready. I wanted to spend the time I needed with them. I quit work when I had them; I'm devoted to them. They know that. They'll be fine." My voice has gotten louder in my defensiveness; the people ahead of me turn slightly around, then away.

Martha blinks, nods slowly. "Well I hope they will be. I really do." She heads back to her airplane suite. I know what she's thinking: I'm too intense. My kids will end up totally neurotic. They'll end up hating me. I know that's what she's thinking. But she's wrong. My kids will end up knowing that they were the priority, that I did not sacrifice their well-being for the sake of some pipe dream, as my mother did. They will end up knowing they came first in my life, always. Of course I miss working. Of course I have days when I literally feel like pulling my hair out. But I stay home, so that my children know if they need me I'm there. I recognize the fact that the need is on my part, too. I see that.

I stare at the man across the aisle from me, asleep with his mouth open, gently snoring. Then I smooth my skirt beneath me, take in a deep breath, reenter that summer day so many years ago when Mrs. O'Donnell moved away.

It turned out I was wrong about our neighbor's house being left absolutely empty. The curtains stayed. But they were open, and late in the afternoon, when the truck pulled away, Sharla and I looked through every window we could reach. Then we sat on Mrs. O'Donnell's back steps, enjoying the mild disorientation of seeing our own yard from there. "She forgot her clothespins," I told Sharla. They were lined up like mournful little soldiers on the gray rope line. I was feeling guilty, thinking we should have had a going-away party for her. But who, other than her cop nephew Leroy, could we have invited? And would that have constituted a party?

Mrs. O'Donnell had called Sharla and me over just before she left, and had given each of us a present wrapped in wrinkled paper. It was left over from Christmas, and featured scenes of Santa Claus that I thought made him look drunk.

We each got one earring of a pair. "This way, you'll always keep in touch with each other," Mrs. O'Donnell said. "You'll have to share, don't you know?" We thanked her profusely and then Leroy came to drive her away. She was wearing a hat and gloves and new black shoes, and looked as dignified as I'd ever seen her. I felt terrible.

"Old Mrs. O'Donnell," I said now. "Poor thing." I
screwed my earring on. It had pearls and rhinestones. I
thought it was pretty, though I also recall thinking that it
didn't really go with anything I had.

"Maybe a window's open and we could crawl in,"
Sharla said, shoving her earring in her front pocket. She
wasn't interested in joining my little memorial service.
She was interested in breaking and entering. It was the
more appealing alternative; I took the earring off and
started to put it in my front pocket, then switched to the
back one—I had to be ever-alert to providing evidence
for Sharla calling me a copycat.

We went around to all the windows again, tried to
open them, found them locked. Then, liking the absur-
dity of it, I went to the front door and knocked loudly,
and the door fell open.

I turned back to Sharla, openmouthed.

"Shut it!" she told me, looking quickly around. Then,
whispering, "We'll come back at midnight."

I loved summer so much. My mother was fixing fried
potatoes for dinner; I could smell them from here. Our
feet were bare and dusty. I had a puffy mosquito bite behind my knee, and itching it gave me a kind of pleasure
that made me close my eyes and lift my chin, like a dog
well-scratched. We were going to Dairy Queen for dessert: Sharla and I favored the coated cones, my mother
got elegant little butterscotch sundaes, and my father
wolfed down entire banana splits. Grasshoppers leaped
up and crisscrossed before us every day; at night the ci-
cadas sang and the sticky June bugs clung to the back
screen door. Homework was as foreign as the red eye of
Mars. Plans fell into your lap, opened as naturally and

exotically as the lotus flower. You could follow an impromptu notion through to its natural end, which is exactly what you were supposed to do with such fine gifts.

"Wake up!" I heard Sharla say. I'd been dreaming a good dream. It concerned a group of fairies who, sorority-like, lived in a castle together. They woke up together, bumped wings as they jostled one another for position at the bathroom sink—equipped with gold fixtures in the shape of swans' heads. When we were younger, it had been the habit of our mother to tell us to go to sleep quickly; that way, the fairies would come sooner to paint stars on our ceiling. I liked believing this was true, and incorporated the notion enough that I often had dreams about those fairies. They were blonde, with the exception of one raven-haired fairy, my favorite, who wore only red and had the look of possible evil in her eyes. The fairies always wore the same thing, sparkly gossamer gowns that tied around their middles with gold ribbon in a crisscross arrangement impossible to duplicate—I had often tried. The only difference between the fairies' gowns was in the color. There was a pale apricot, a bright yellow, a dusky purple, and many shades of blue. And red, of course, a red so deep it neared black in the small valleys of the folds. The gowns trailed off at the end as though someone had set about erasing them from the bottom up, but then had gotten distracted and gone away. You could not see shoes, or feet; only the disappearing edges of a fantasy.

In my dream, I'd been given a large gold key to unlock the fairies' closet door. It was a high, white cabinet, trimmed with gold. I opened the door, then stood before a line of their gowns, the sparkles winking at me. I could not believe my nearness. I had just reached out a hand to touch them when Sharla got through to me.

"Let's *go!*" she whispered harshly. "Why are you sleeping?"

This seemed a dumb question. I didn't answer it. Instead, I sat up and straightened my T-shirt and underpants as though I were preparing to leave for work, which I suppose I was.

"You have to wear your robe," Sharla said. She was wearing hers, and she handed me mine. It was a white quilted thing, with rhinestone buttons. It was just like Sharla's, only smaller. We hated our robes. They were a gift from our grandmother, our mother's mother, who always sent us clothes we hated. She did not understand us, we felt. And she would call us from her home in New York the day after we had received whatever she sent and we were expected to go on and on about it. "Did you notice the buttons?" she'd asked about the robe.

"They're very pretty," I'd responded dutifully. Actually, I did like the buttons. But not there. I wanted to use them for something else. Eyes in a voodoo doll I intended to make, for example. I needed someone else's hair for that, though. I was waiting to cut Sharla's when she was sleeping, but the occasion hadn't presented itself, because so far, when she was sleeping, I was sleeping, too. I was waiting for her to get sick.

"Why do we have to wear robes?" I asked.

"Because it's someone else's house, dummy."

"But it's empty!"

"Be quiet, or we'll get caught." She cupped her hands around my ear, whispered into it, "You can't be in your underwear in someone else's house. Just put your robe on. Let's *go.*"

I was hungry, I realized suddenly. I wanted to eat something before I went to work. But Sharla, walking before me with her back ramrod straight, was going to be in no mood for dillydallying. Still, when we passed through the kitchen on the way to the front door, I opened a cupboard and grabbed the first thing I felt, which was a bag of marshmallows. A good choice, and a lucky one.

The moon was full and bright white; you could have read by it. I stowed this information away; next time, we would do that, bring out books and read by the light of the moon. They would need to be the right books, of course. Ones about witches, say, or magazine love stories with plenty of kissing scenes. You could find them in the *Ladies' Home Journal*, complete with illustrations. The women always had their red lips parted; the mens' heads bowed low, moving toward the women in perpetuity. A wind was always blowing, so as to arrange the women's hair in wild and irresistible styles.

Outside Mrs. O'Donnell's door I felt a sudden rush of fear. "What if someone else is in there?" I asked. The door had been left open. For many hours. And though the moon was bright, the inside of the house was dark enough for misdeeds.

"Who would be in there?" Sharla asked, in the tired voice she reserved for telling me I was a moron. However, I noticed her hand stayed still on the doorknob.

"A hobo," I said, and nearly saw him then, toothless and leering, sitting in a corner of Mrs. O'Donnell's poor, empty bedroom. His handkerchief was off its stick and lay open before him; he was unpacked, claiming the space as his own. He had BO. And in the slatted light that came through Mrs. O'Donnell's left-behind venetian blinds, you could see a knife clenched in his hairy fist. I imagined the Swiss army variety like our father's, only not as nice. Rusty. In the habit of opening windpipes rather than bottles of grape soda.

"There are no hobos in Clear Falls," Sharla said.

"How do you know?"

"What is the matter with you? Don't you want to do this?"

"Yes!" Maybe not.

"There is no one in there. It is an empty house that we get to explore for as long as we want." She squinted at me. "What's under your arm?"

"Marshmallows."

At first, she looked as though she might yell at me again; but then she held out her hand. I gave her one; then, as she did not take her hand back, two more. She shoved them in her mouth, then opened the door. And there it was, the exact smell of Mrs. O'Donnell. A warm smell, like ironing, mixed with something like old orange peels. "Shhh!" Sharla said, closing the door behind me. She stood perfectly still, her head cocked, listening.

"What are you doing?" I said.

"Shhhhhhhhhhhhhh!!!"

I had gotten to her. She was making sure there wasn't a hobo. My pride made me smile; I ate another marshmallow. We were a team, equal in importance, never mind the age difference.

Sharla turned to glare at me; apparently I was making noise eating.

"No one's here," I said loudly, in my marshmallow-thickened voice. "Tut-tut, chicken-butt."

And then I led the way, *I* did, across the empty living room and into the center of the tiny dining room.

"This was the dining room," I said solemnly.

"I know that."

"You weren't ever in here."

"I was, too."

"When?"

"Once when you were sick; I borrowed some soup from her. Mom sent me. She gave me a can of tomato soup."

"I *ate* it?" I thought of Mrs. O'Donnell's bumpy knuckles reaching in her cupboard for soup to give to me, shivered a little in regretful repulsion. It occurred to me that she would never make soup again. I wondered what she had done with the food left in her house on moving day. Maybe she'd given it to Leroy. Or set it out in her metal trash can, which now waited at the curb looking a bit splendid—such was the power of the moonlight.

"Let's go look in her bedroom," Sharla said.

I was going to say that nothing was there, but it wasn't true. There *was* something there; there was something everywhere. There was a spirit in the house, a sad sense of someone newly gone. Each room had its own small, untold lament. The dining room missed its lace table-cloth and the turkey dinners Mrs. O'Donnell had served when her husband was alive. The kitchen tap dripped, looking for macaroni to rinse. The air in the bedroom would be rich with the leftovers from Mrs. O'Donnell's dreams and her middle-of-the-night wakenings, those times when she sat on the edge of the bed with her hands on her knees, her thin hair wild about her glasses-less face, the ticking of her bedside clock suddenly loud. I was sure she'd sat like that. I was sure everyone did that, once they got old.

We climbed the stairs, walked down the hall past the bathroom, and Sharla pushed open the door to the empty square that had been Mrs. O'Donnell's bedroom. I was right; the air here was charged. I felt the hairs on my arms lift; an invisible finger zipped up my spine. I looked at Sharla, wanting to ask if she felt all this, too, but her face was closed, impassive. She wasn't colliding with memories of a life lived and now gone; she was simply looking around. The closet door was half open; the white curtains at the window hung still as stone. There were little white balls hanging from the edges of the curtains. "Look," I told Sharla. "The surrey with the fringe on top."

"What?"

"The curtains," I said. "The surrey with the fringe on top."

"Don't be stupid."

I ate a marshmallow, weighed the fairness of her remark.

Right.

"She slept so many nights here," I said.

"I know." Sharla's voice was quiet and mournful. Now I was on the right track.

"She was so nice," I sighed. Salt to the wound, an occasional specialty of mine.

"Not really," Sharla said, her reverie broken.

"Uh-huh!"

"Oh, you're just saying that because she's gone."

"Nuh-uh."

"Uh-*huh*!"

"Be quiet," I said. "The cops will come, and you're only in your robe."

Sharla went toward the bathroom; I started to follow, then went my own way, into the spare bedroom. Pink curtains here, ruffled edges. An outline on the floor of where the braided rug used to be, I remembered it. I felt Sharla come in behind me.

"What was this?" she asked.

"The guest room. There was a little bed, right here; it was brown wood, with a pink bedspread. And a plant was on the bedside stand, I think it was a sweet-potato plant. Or . . . I don't know, maybe an African violet."

How important things had become, now that they were gone! I felt a sudden panic that I would soon forget everything. Mrs. O'Donnell's face would be a blur, surrounded by her perm. And then the memory of the perm itself . . . gone? The trajectory of this line of thought was making me nervous. I told myself the plant had definitely been an African violet; I made myself see the fuzzy white on the leaves, the slight tilt of them toward the sun. I saw one shy purple blossom bent toward the earth it lived in.

Sharla leaned against the wall. "The guest room, huh? She never had any guests."

"I know."

A troubled silence.

Then, "Want another marshmallow?" I asked.

"How can you eat at a time like this?"

"She would want us to," I said, though I was not at all sure of this.

I left the guest room, went downstairs, and sat in the middle of the living-room floor. You could sit anywhere now; nothing was in the way of anything. I rather liked that.

Sharla came down soon afterward. We finished the marshmallows, then lay on the floor head to head, limbs stretched out like snow angels. "How would you decorate this room if it was your house?" Sharla asked.

My house? My *house*? All of it—a kitchen, a bathroom, two bedrooms, a back-porch stoop, a front door with a mail slot?

"I don't know," I said.

"Me neither."

We sighed, exactly together, it seemed to me, and this was deeply comforting. I had a thought to take Sharla's hand, but I knew she'd frown and lightly slap me away. We were deeply connected, Sharla and I, but very different. I was a cuddler; Sharla looked at an embrace as imprisonment. I could not touch her except to brush her hair, she liked that. In fact, she would pay me to do it. She would give me a Betty and Veronica comic book, or perhaps use of her charm bracelet for half an hour, though I had to wash and dry it before returning it to her. "You have a habit of being sticky," she told me. And then, when shame filled my face, "It's nothing *bad*; it's just messy."

Eventually, we rose and toured Mrs. O'Donnell's empty house one more time—wordlessly agreeing to exclude the basement. Then we left, pulling the door shut behind us. We slept out in the yard for a while, then went in. Again, we hadn't been missed. It was becoming boring, getting away with so much. Soon, we would need to up the ante.

* * *

When I awakened the next morning, I was seized by the fear that we had left fingerprints behind, unique lines of us captured in marshmallow dust. I thought we should sneak back in and get rid of the evidence. But it was too late. Outside my bedroom window I saw that another moving van had pulled up. And standing beside it was the raven-haired fairy of my dreams, only you could see her feet. They were wearing the highest heels I'd ever seen. Under the fullest skirt. Which was red, but softened by large white polka dots. Her short-sleeved sweater was all red, though, as was a scarf she had tied around her neck. Her belt was black patent leather, cinched tightly around her tiny waist.

Sharla was already up by the time I came downstairs, standing watching at the living-room window, eating a bowl of Cheerios and sliced peaches. "Look who's moving in," she said, her mouth full. And then she said something unintelligible.

"Is later?" I asked.

Sharla swallowed. "Liz *Tay*lor," she said. "I swear to God."

I looked. I saw the resemblance. For a moment, I wondered if it were true. But this couldn't be Liz Taylor. I had seen Liz recently in *Photoplay*, and her hair was short. This woman's black hair hung down to the middle of her back. And a silver/black German shepherd lay beside her. Liz would have poodles, I was sure of it. They all did, in Hollywood.

My mother came into the room. "Stop *spy*ing!" she said, then came to the window herself. "Oh," she said. "Well. My goodness." And then, "Well, they certainly have some nice antiques. Oh, look at that, a brass bed. Wouldn't I love to have that!"

"When do we meet her?" I asked. Every light on my console was lit.

"Well . . ." My mother's brow furrowed; she wiped her hands absentmindedly on her apron. It was a new one, made out of a towel with blue and green geometric shapes.

"I suppose we could invite them to supper," she said. "They won't have any time for cooking today. And I'll make *her* a little coffee to put in the thermos right now. You girls can bring it to her."

"I'll carry it," Sharla said.

I could never beat her. "Front seat/by the door/called it/no changes!" she'd say, before the words were fully out of my parents' mouths that we were going somewhere in the car. What Sharla never thought about, though, was that the ride home was often longer. It could pay to bide your time, to hold out for a chance at winning something later that would be better than what was offered now.

I hear the *bong* of the FASTEN SEAT BELT sign, look down, and see that mine is not secured. I have a thought to leave it unhooked, just to see if I get caught. But then a flight attendant appears, leans in toward me. "You need to fasten your seat belt," she says quietly, as though to spare me from embarrassment.

"I *was*," I say, and the words sound petulant, as though they are coming from a child. "But thank you!" I add, too late; the attendant is several rows up. She's moving quickly, trying to get to her own seat; the plane has begun to buck like a bronco.

People laugh nervously—something about this seems pretend, even ridiculous—and then it is remarkably silent. I clutch the armrests, get mad at my mother all over again, because now she might be responsible for my death. But then the flight becomes abruptly smooth; people gradually begin conversing, and then we are all back to normal.

The flight attendant starts down the aisle again, smiling. She's quite overweight, especially for a flight attendant, and I like that. For one thing, it makes me think she's a lot more capable than the thin ones. In the event of an emergency, give me somebody who can pick me up.

For a brief time, Sharla wanted to be a flight attendant—
"stewardesses," they were called then. When she was a
senior in high school, someone from the airlines came
out to the house to meet her, sat beside her on the sofa in
the living room with his closed briefcase on his lap. In the
end, Sharla was judged not pretty enough, though it was
presented to her in a much more tactful way in a letter
she received a week later. Georgia and my father were in-
censed; I was secretly happy. I didn't want Sharla to be
flying away all the time; I didn't want anyone going away.
"She's every bit as pretty as any stewardess *I've* ever seen!"
my father said. I wasn't sure. I'd flown only a couple of
times, on family vacations, but the stewardesses I saw
then were remarkably pretty: the kind of women you
wanted to stare and stare at. It was the kind of beauty
Jasmine Johnson had, though her beauty had a dark, pulling side that could make you uncomfortable, that could
make you feel you were falling helplessly toward someplace you weren't at all sure you wanted to go.

I pull the window shade down a bit to block out some
of the bright sun, see that we're directly over the center
of a huge lake. It's so far down, that lake. I'll bet it's
really deep. I think about the blackness of the deepest
parts of the ocean, the sightless creatures that live there,
and feel an internal slump of discouragement. I know
those creatures don't mind not seeing. But I mind for
them. I want them to surface and see everything.

"**I**'m Jasmine Johnson," our new neighbor said, when Sharla and I presented ourselves with the thermos of coffee. Her voice was low and melodic; it reminded me of Peggy Lee singing "Fever." "Please call me Jasmine," she added, smiling.

Jasmine! Her name was as exotic as her appearance—I visualized it written in gold, with ornate curlicues. When it came time to introduce myself, I used the formal "Virginia." Sharla looked askance at me, but did not begin snorting and pointing at me, saying, "Nuh-*uh*, her name's just *Ginny*!" which is what I'd feared. I was already embarrassed about the container the coffee was in; we'd used my plain lunch-box thermos because we couldn't find the more elegant silver one we used on car trips. "I don't see it anywhere," my mother had said, her voice muffled because her head was stuck far inside one of the lower cabinets. Then, emerging and using her fingers to fluff back her mussed-up hair, "It's too big anyway. She wouldn't know what to do with all that coffee."

"We could have some with her," I'd said, and earned a sharp poke in the ribs from Sharla.

"You girls don't drink coffee," my mother had said, her lips a prim straight line. "Not until you are twenty-one."

Well, not in front of her. But we drank coffee all right, every chance we got. Once, when our parents went out, we made and drank a whole pot. "Look how much it makes me *pee*!" Sharla had yelled in her hepped-up voice from behind the closed bathroom door. And I, waiting desperately for my own turn, had yelled back, "I *know*!"

Every night after supper, when we did the dishes, Sharla and I finished the coffee that was left in our parents' cups. We fought silently over who got my mother's—she used more sugar. We never simply added sugar ourselves; I think we believed it would be pressing our luck. Suppose one of our parents walked in when we were stirring? My father would sit us down at the kitchen table for one of his low-voiced lectures about age-appropriate activities and then impose some irritating punishment like early bedtimes for a week, mostly for the benefit of our mother. She tended to enlarge small crimes and to take them personally. After we'd misbehaved, she would sit in the living room in her small blue velvet chair, looking out the window and periodically shaking her head. The day she caught us chicken-calling a teacher we particularly disliked, she actually wept a little. "*Mom!*" Sharla had said, and my mother had waved her hand in pouty dismissal. "You have no idea what this suggests about your upbringing," she told us. "No idea." We were made to call and apologize, while my mother stood nearby, supervising. Sharla went first, as usual, leaving me to cast about for something to say that was not too close to her apology. In the end, however, I copied her exactly. "Sorry, we didn't really mean anything by it," I said.

"Oh, I know you didn't," Mrs. Mennafee said. "As I just told your sister, I used to make calls like that myself." I had a thought to ask her to tell that to my mother, but instead I went with Sharla to sit for forty-five minutes in our bedroom, part two of our punishment. It wasn't awful; I was in need of a nap anyway. We got out in time to watch *The Mickey Mouse Club*, a vast relief since I was in love with Jimmy. My only chance to get him was to communicate telepathically. I stared at his wavy, black-and-white image, saying over and over in my mind, "I love you; I am ready." Sharla favored the goofy boys, with their too-big teeth; I knew a real man when I saw one, Jimmy's mouse ears notwithstanding.

Jasmine bent to accept the thermos of coffee from Sharla, and I smelled her perfume. I found it extraordinary that someone would wear perfume in the middle of the day, and on moving day besides. Once, in Monroe's department store, I'd seen a small container of Chanel No. 5 that was called "purse size," but I'd thought it was a kind of joke. Who would carry perfume in their purse? Here was someone who would.

"Come on in," Jasmine said, and we followed her into the house. There were boxes everywhere, but she went without hesitation to one in the dining room, stripped the tape from it, reached in and pulled out one cup, then two more. She spaced them evenly on top of a smaller box, sat on the floor beside it, and then looked up at us expectantly.

"We don't drink coffee," I said, and was elbowed again.

"No?" Her black eyebrows were raised into pretty arches.

"We do sometimes," Sharla said. "When it's a special occasion."

"Well, this certainly qualifies," Jasmine said, and filled each cup. Then, holding hers up, "Here's to new beginnings."

We sat on either side of her at our cardboard table, and lifted our cups to tap against one another. They were fancy flowered things, the kind of dishes my mother used at Thanksgiving and Christmas and would not let us carry unless it was one at a time. But Jasmine handled them as casually as though they were plastic bathroom cups. I noticed Sharla's little finger was lifted ever so slightly; I did the same.

"So," Sharla said. "Do you have any kids?"

Jasmine shook her head. "No, I'm not married."

My eyes widened.

"You mean you're going to live here all alone?" Sharla asked. My question exactly, though it would have taken a while for me to get around to asking it.

Jasmine smiled. "Well, I won't be lonely. I'll have you two for friends, right?"

"Right," I said quickly.

"Miss?" one of the movers called. "Coats. Where do you want them?"

"Which ones?" Jasmine asked.

The man read the writing on the box. " 'Winter,' it says. 'Minks.' And . . . looks like . . . 'P. lamb'?"

"Oh, right," she said. "In the basement, I guess."

Minks? *Minks????* The things I had to talk to Sharla about were beginning to make my teeth ache. She felt the same; I could see it in the wildness of her eyes. As soon as Jasmine agreed to come to our house that night for dinner, we fled to our bedroom—this after we told our mother that the guest list numbered one, due to the fact that the new neighbor was not married. "Is that right?" my mother said. She cleared her throat, stared past us. Then she headed for her cookbook shelf.

Sharla flopped on her bed, put her pillow over her stomach. I lay down, too, stuck my hand inside the waistband of my shorts, sighed in happy anticipation of the juicy talk we were about to have.

"Quit!" Sharla said suddenly, nastily.

"What?"

"Get your hand out of your pants, you retard."

"I don't have my hand in my pants."

She stared hard at the vicinity in question, shook her head rapidly from side to side to emphasize the fact that she *was* staring hard. It looked like her eyeballs were jiggling. I laughed.

She sat up, angry. "You think that's funny? To pick at your butt?"

"I'm *not*!" I said, angry myself now. "My shorts are too tight! I just put my hand here to relax my waist!"

"Well, that's not how it looks." Sharla lay back down, stared at the ceiling. "It looks like a retard. I hope you don't do that in school."

"I'm sure."

We waited together for silence to restore our moods. Finally, "I dreamed I was a bachelor in my Maidenform bra," I ventured.

Sharla raised one leg into the air, turned her ankle this way and that. She kept threatening to get an ankle bracelet, even though my mother disallowed them, calling them cheap-looking. "Bachelor*ette*," she said. "Huh. We have *never* had one of *those* on this street."

"Ha!" I said. "We have never had one in this *neigh-* borhood. Probably not in this whole town!"

"How do you know?"

"Name one time you ever heard of one."

Sharla thought. "There *could* be one in the *town*," she said finally. She began picking at the edges of her pillow. I liked how she did this; it made the pillow seem more than it was. I felt the urge to do it myself, but suppressed it. Then Sharla said, "But probably not, this is not the town for bachelorettes."

"What is?"

"They like New York City and gay Paree."

"Did you hear what that moving man said? She has a mink coat!"

"I know!" Sharla said. "And she was sooooo casual about it, like oh yawn, how boring, fur coats."

"Well, that is the sign of a truly rich person," I said. "They are always casual about things like that."

"How do you know? What do you know about rich people?"

"Never mind, I just know some things," I said, with such authority that Sharla didn't argue—I did read much more than she did. Instead, she said, "I wonder if she has a boyfriend."

"Ho, not one. More like a million of them."

Silence. I could see Sharla imagining such a thing. I imagined it as well, created in my mind a long line of men snaking down the sidewalk outside Jasmine's house, all of them dressed in tuxedos, all with black hair slicked back wetly. They carried bouquets of flowers, fancy candy, black velvet boxes holding dazzling pieces of jewelry. They looked neither to the left nor to the right. They were selectively blind, focused only on their desire.

Sharla turned onto her side, pushed her hair back from her face, then over one eye. "If she takes the bedroom Mrs. O'Donnell used, we'll be able to see it from the bathroom."

"I know."

"Want to go look and see if we can tell yet?"

We vied for position at the bathroom window, keeping our heads low. And suddenly there Jasmine was, standing with her back to us, showing the men where to put a huge dresser. It was placed opposite the brass bed.

"I think she has good taste," I whispered.

"I know."

"I wonder why she chose *that* house."

"Beats me."

Jasmine turned around then, looked out of her window right into ours, and we were caught. Sharla ducked down, but I stayed where I was, red-faced. Jasmine smiled, then waved. I waved back.

"Get down; get *down*!" Sharla whispered, between clenched teeth.

"It's okay," I said. "She sees us. She doesn't care."

From downstairs came the scent of butter melting. My mother was making something special.

"Girls?" she called up.

We went out into the hall, called down to answer her.

"Would you run over to Sullivan's and get me some mushrooms? See if he has some fresh ones."

It was Bella Vista chicken, then. Probably she'd make her Viennese torte cake, too, and ring the plate with fresh flowers before she served it. She only did things like this when company came. If she did it for our family, our father and Sharla made gentle fun of her. I actually liked my mother's creativity in such matters, but did not want to admit it, in case Sharla and my father were right.

I imagined we'd be eating in the dining room, and when we came downstairs, I saw it was so. The heavy, cream-colored tablecloth already lay on the table, the one my parents got as a wedding gift. Their initials were monogrammed at one end, edges linked together. Normally, my mother put those initials at the hostess end, closest to the kitchen. Today, though, they were facing out. They were what you saw as soon as you entered the room.

A few rows ahead of me, I hear two children, a brother and sister, about eight or nine years old, talking. The girl says, "I love it when we get so high and we're out of the world."

"We're not out of the world," the boy says.

A long pause. Then the girl says, "Glen. Yes, we are. We are in the sky."

"No, stupid," Glen says. "When you are in outer *space*, you are out of the world."

"So? Space is sky, isn't it?"

Glen thinks. So do I.

I love listening to conversations between children. I often change seats on a bus or an airplane to be near them. Right after takeoff, I heard this same girl say, "When we get up real high, I'm going to open a window and see where we *really* are." And Glen, pointing at the blocklike illustration on the flight-attendant call button, observed, "Boy. They don't *draw* good."

My idea of hell is to be stuck on a long flight in front of loud-talking businessmen holding an impromptu air-meeting, each trying to outdo the other using the mind-numbing vocabulary of the profit-oriented. "Why must you *talk* about this?" I always want to ask them. "Don't you see that it doesn't matter at all?" Of course it does matter; it just doesn't matter to me. I married a man who teaches English at a small college. We are not rich, but when my husband talks to me about his job, my eyes don't glaze over.

I wonder now what my mother must have felt when my father talked about his work—he was a small businessman. She never had that glazed-eye expression, but she never offered much in the way of response, either: a smile, perhaps. A light touch to the back of his collar before she rose from the table for more green beans.

She was different from other mothers, in many ways. On the plus side, her artistic abilities made her able to assist wonderfully well with certain kinds of homework. She helped me with colored pencil drawings of wildflowers, and birds, and maps; and she made perfect finishing touches to a papier-mâché human heart that I entered in a science fair. Once she helped me too much with an art project I was given to do over a long weekend when I was in fifth grade. It was a watercolor of a Mexican woman making bread that ended up on permanent display in the entryway of our school. It must have been obvious that it was not really my work, but the teacher loved the painting so much she did nothing but give me an A+ for it, and then make arrangements for it to be seen by everyone who walked into the school. My name was in small print at the corner of the painting. The art teacher's name was put below the painting, in print significantly larger.

The woman in that painting was wearing a long, faded blue dress, belted by a red and yellow woven tie. Her feet were bare against large, uneven tiles. She wore fat braids tied with fraying pieces of string. There were many lovely things about that painting: young as I was, I appreciated the quality of light, the richness in the colors. But what was most intriguing was the woman's face. You could not really see it; her gaze was directed down into the wooden bread bowl and slightly away. Yet somehow you knew exactly what that face looked like. You knew because of the slump of the shoulders, the resignation in the hands that worked at less than they were capable of. My mother could do that, render a strong feeling with a few strokes of a Number 2 pencil. It was a gift that always surprised people; it made us proud.

On the negative side, you often had the feeling that something dark and uneasy was going on with my mother; but she would not acknowledge it, nor allow anyone else to. After Jasmine moved in, that internal storm grew fiercer and fiercer in my mother, eventually leading her to make a decision that must have felt inevitable, if astoundingly painful. I wonder how much of that pain she predicted, and how much of it was a black surprise. I didn't much care, then, about the pain there was for her in leaving. Even now, if the truth be told, I am mainly just curious.

On the night Jasmine first came to our house for dinner, the doorbell rang promptly at six o'clock. I opened it to see her standing there, holding a bottle of wine. A thin strand of lavender ribbon tied blue flowers onto the neck of the bottle. Those flowers grew all over Mrs. O'Donnell's backyard, though now it occurred to me that it was Jasmine's yard. I couldn't remember Mrs. O'Donnell ever picking them, though.

"Thank you for coming," I said. "What lovely flowers. Shall I put them in water?" These were exact lines from a movie I'd recently seen. I loved how well they worked for me now.

"Pardon?"

"The flowers. Want them in water?"

She looked at them. "Oh! Oh no, they're just for decoration."

"Well." I shrugged. It seemed a sin to use flowers that way, to pick them and then just let them die. Of course a greater sin would be to communicate my disapproval of anything a guest did.

But Jasmine guessed my thoughts. "Unless you'd *like* to save them," she said. "It might be nice, actually."

"I have an aspirin bottle. We can use that." I'd stashed an empty bottle of orange-flavored children's aspirin in

50

my nightstand drawer, because my mother said we weren't going to use it anymore, we'd gotten old enough for adult aspirin. I'd wanted the comfort of the smell nearby, just in case. "Please come in," I told Jasmine.

She had changed out of her red outfit and into a blue one—a simple dress, deep pockets cut on the diagonal, cuffed short sleeves with white buttons at the ends, a white cardigan sweater over her shoulders. Her shoes were still high heels, I was happy to see. Blue ones. I hadn't known they made those. Her hair was up in a fat French twist. She wore pearl earrings.

"Mom!" I called. "Our guest is here!"

My mother came into the room. "Oh, I'm sorry," she said. "I didn't hear the bell. I had the radio on, and what with the banging of all the pots and pans . . ." She held her hand out. "I'm Marion Eastman."

"Jasmine Johnson." She shook my mother's hand, smiled at her in a way I thought suggested some kind of familiarity. They might have been old friends who thought they had forgotten about each other, but no! now they were meeting again and they remembered everything. They remembered every thing. I saw that my mother was nervous, and this was interesting to me. I'd seen her nervous around men, but never around another woman.

I lean my head back against the airplane seat, stare at the ceiling. In pulling forth these memories from so long ago, I see how much I actually saw then. And how much I denied seeing. It's a curious thing how that works, how elaborately and unconsciously careful we are to protect our most delicate parts. Instinctively, the spider spins the web; just as automatically, the human shields the heart.

People always told me I was perceptive. From the time I started school, teachers would mention it on my report cards, on papers I wrote. For a while, I considered using what I was told was a talent to become a psychologist, even a psychiatrist. But I didn't want to learn any more about human nature than I knew already. If I am completely honest, which I am trying very hard to be right now, I would say that it was not just that I decided my career would be my children. Rather it occurs to me that I did not pursue any profession having to do with psychology because if I understood more about how people work, how they are, I might understand my mother. And I did not want to understand my mother. If I understood her, I might have to forgive her. And at some critical time I became very much invested in not forgiving her—we all did. It became an underpinning in our reduced family, a need, even; just as there seems to be a terrible need for family feuds to continue. In a way, it is as if your refusal to forgive is too much a part of you for you to lose it. Who would you be without it? Not yourself. Lost, somehow. Think of how people tend to pick the same chair to sit in over and over again. We are always trying to make sure we know where we are. Though we may long for adventure, we also cherish the familiar. We just do.

The night after Jasmine came to dinner, Sharla and I lay on our quilt outside. Overhead, the sky was thick with clouds that were black and roiling. We were waiting for the lightning to come and scare us a little; then we'd go inside. So far, there had only been the low rumble of thunder, a sound more like a complaint than a threat. We were sharing the last piece of torte; the nearly empty plate lay exactly between us.

"Do you think Mom likes Jasmine?" I asked.

"I don't know."

I scooped some whipped cream onto my finger. "Does Dad?"

"*Yeah!*"

"How do you know?"

"How could you not know?" Sharla picked up the plate, licked it. Well, that was that; the torte was gone for sure now. Sharla's tongue was long and lizardlike; she could touch her nose with it.

"He liked her, all right; his eyeballs were practically bugging out of his head."

"Nuh-uh," I said. She was disgusting, Sharla.

"Uh-*huh*."

"He did not hardly even talk to her."

54

Sharla picked a handful of grass, smelled it, flung it out before her. It spread apart like low fireworks. She sighed.

"Man. You are really stupid."

"Why?"

"That's how men are when they really feel something; they don't say one word."

I considered this. My father did grow silent at times of great emotion. Once, when I was narrowly missed by a speeding car in a movie parking lot, my mother yanked me out of harm's way, burst into tears, and began talking a mile a minute about how I had to watch *out*, how some people had no *bus*iness having a license, how *close* that was, how *awful* it would have been. . . . My father picked me up and held me. I saw him close his eyes, heard him breathe in deep, smelled his Old Spice. That was all.

"But you don't think Mom likes her?"

"I didn't say that. I said I don't know."

"I think she does."

"Why do you care so much if Mom likes her?"

"Well, they're neighbors," I said, though that wasn't it, that wasn't why I was interested in them liking each other. I wanted free access to Jasmine Johnson. I didn't want anyone asking me about going over there, or, worse, disallowing it.

A vein of lightning lit the sky spectacularly; there was a split-second sensation of someone turning on a too-bright overhead light. Sharla and I held our breath and counted. It took only two seconds for the thunder to follow. I felt the first fat raindrop land directly in the center of my forehead.

"Here it comes," Sharla said.

"I know," I answered.

When we got inside, we found our mother standing in the kitchen.

"All right, how long have you been sneaking out like this?" she asked, her voice quiet but shaking.

We didn't answer, either of us.

"Go to your room," she said, and we did.

I felt bad. I hated seeing her react with such sad calm to something she was really upset about. And I wondered why everything she felt, she felt so hard.

The next day was Thursday, Culture Day. This is what my mother called it. Monday was Vocabulary Day, when each member of the family was obliged to bring a new word to the dinner table; Tuesday was Current Events Day, and you better have had a look at the headlines. Wednesday was Correspondence Day, and we sat with our mother at the dining-room table after dinner to write our grandparents and whomever else we might choose (we chose no one else, ever). Friday was International Day, when my mother presented us with such things as Mexican enchiladas, Italian spaghetti, or, her weakest entry to date, store-bought French bread. As far as I could tell, the only difference between it and our regular bread was the shape, plus the cartoon drawing on the bag of a man wearing a beret and a pencil-thin mustache.

But Thursday was Culture Day. Sharla took piano lessons; I went to ballet class at Yvette's Studio for the Dance. Though I enjoyed looking at ballerinas, I hated studying ballet. It was the crowns the ballerinas wore that I lusted after, the ride in the elaborately decorated sleigh I saw when we watched *The Nutcracker* on television. I had no desire to train my body to do difficult things requiring grace and precision. I was the worst in class, so awful I wasn't even made fun of. My instructor, a painfully thin, soft-spoken woman who wore cardigan sweaters with fraying sleeves over her hopeful little tutus, tried valiantly to teach me the most basic things, but it was no good. I could not remember sequences of steps, and I was amazingly clumsy. It seemed ridiculous to me to clomp around holding my arms up over my head, fingers arranged into what was supposed to be graceful asymmetry but in fact resembled rigor mortis. I felt like an elephant in a wading pool.

"Well," Yvette would say each week in her sweet French accent, "I can see zat you 'ave maybe impouv." We both knew she was lying. I saw sadness in her large brown eyes; I wasn't sure for whom. Over and over, I had tried to explain to my mother that I was no good at dance, that I did not enjoy it. "You're not there to enjoy it," she always said. And when I would ask her what I was there for, she would say, "Never mind. Later on, you'll be glad I made you go."

This was the same line of reasoning she used on Sharla, more or less. Sharla hated piano even more than I hated ballet, and I didn't blame her. At least I could stand at the side of the classroom, daydreaming, for much of the time I was in the dance studio. For an entire hour, Sharla had to sit right beside the infamous Mrs. Beatrice Eaton, whose horrible breath was not aided by the ancient peppermint candy she kept in a flowered tin in her man's briefcase. She was a fat woman, proof positive that fat does not equal jolly, with a chin that looked like a small pocketbook. Her face was covered with an orangish powder that occasionally dropped in small flecks like glitter onto her black clothes. She had a red plastic ruler that she used for rapping Sharla's knuckles when she made a mistake twice in a row. My mother had complained about this, had at one point told Mrs. Eaton that she would be fired if she continued to do it. "Oh, for heaven's sake, Marion, it's only a *tap*," she told my mother. "Music is about *dis*cipline. Surely you *know* that."

"Well, I'm sure it is," my mother said, not sure at all— Sharla and I, eavesdropping in the kitchen, heard the doubt in her voice. But her uncertainty dropped away when she said, "However, in this house we don't believe in striking children."

"Well," Mrs. Eaton said, in a half-swallowed way that suggested certain children could do with a strike. And then, "All right, I will try, Marion; but I must tell you it is not good practice to interfere with creative methodology. I can't work well with parents hanging over me. Who knows what is being quashed in your daughter if you don't let me draw on my own artistic resources—and Sharla's."

She had my mother there, and she knew it. My mother believed that creative talent lay huge but latent in us. One of her jobs, she felt, was to unleash it. Given the natural constraints of a very small town (Mrs. Eaton, for example, was the one and only piano teacher within a forty-mile radius), she was doing the best she could. Our abiding consolation was that on Culture Day we could also pick whatever dessert we wanted. Crêpes suzette, we once demanded, having heard about them some-where, and my mother presented us that night with pancakes topped with cherry jelly and whipped cream. When we asked for baked Alaska, she served mounds of lightly browned meringue over a scoop of Neapolitan ice cream. We didn't believe these dishes were authentic, but they were close enough. And we loved our mother for trying. And for just about everything else as well. That's how it was, then.

When I got up one morning, I found a note from my mother on the kitchen table. "Next door," it said. I knew which "next door" she meant. She would not be at Suzy Lindemeyer's house; she didn't really care for Mrs. Lindemeyer. My mother called her "Mrs. Five Operations" because her various surgeries were all Mrs. Lindemeyer ever wanted to talk about. Even to us. "My hysterectomy scar is about to drive me right out of my mind," she had confided to us the week before, when we helped carry her groceries in. "Itchy? Lord, you have no idea!" And then, her eyes somewhat playful but mostly needy, "Would you like to see it?"

"No, ma'am," Sharla said quickly and fled without her fifty cents.

"Maybe later," I said. "We have to go now."

I awakened Sharla and told her our mother was at Jasmine Johnson's house. "Huh," Sharla said sleepily. "Really?"

We ate Oreos for breakfast, followed by spaghetti left over from last night's dinner, and the usual Coke floats. Then we headed for the backyard, garbed in our Indian dresses. "I'm going to make medicine from flowers today," I said.

"What do you mean?" Sharla asked. And then, "Wipe

that tomato sauce from the corner of your mouth. It looks like blood."

"Maybe I just ate a dead animal," I said. "Raw."

"You are sick."

"They did that!"

"Not hardly."

"Yes they did, I read it."

"They cooked, you idiot. They had fire."

I said nothing, blinked.

"They had *spits*," Sharla said.

"Oh yeah. Well, not cavemen, they didn't."

"Who do you think *discovered* fire? And we are not even doing cavemen."

"Who cares?" I said, and headed into the woods. "The Indians did make medicine from flowers, for the heart, and that's what I'm doing." It occurred to me that I didn't care if Sharla came with me or not. I straightened inside my own skin, taller.

At one in the afternoon, my mother had still not returned from Jasmine's house. Sharla and I, irritable at not having any ideas for forbidden things to do, lay on the floor of our room, rubbing ice cubes over our foreheads, in the crooks of our elbows, behind our knees. It was ninety-seven degrees. Our shorts and sleeveless blouses stuck to us.

"Want to snoop in their dresser drawers?" I asked.

She didn't answer.

"Sharla?"

"*What?*" She could get so nasty when she got hot. You couldn't say a word to her.

"Do you want to *snoop*?"

She looked at me, then away. "We just did it last week. Anyway, there's nothing."

It was true that we had not yet found anything great. The closest we came to something interesting was the time we found the photograph of a woman at the bottom of my father's underwear drawer. She was beautiful— curly golden hair, big blue eyes, deep dimples. She wore a yellow collared sweater, open at the throat for as far down as the picture went. "Hi, Handsome!" was written at the corner. And then, "All my love to you, Heidi, June, 1941." This horrified and intrigued us. We discussed it nightly, and then, a few days later, we began pestering our mother about her old boyfriends, hoping we could segue into my father's old girlfriends. This did not happen. My mother, warming to the idea of letting us know she was at one time a pretty hot ticket, settled into a kitchen chair and gave us details we didn't want to know about her relationship with Peter Barnes. He played quarterback on her high school football team. He made a path of violets down her front sidewalk for her to walk on out to his car when he took her to the senior prom. Gave her a purple orchid that night, too; his father was a rich man. My mother fingered the dust cloth on her lap as though it were her corsage, offered to her once again from dreamland.

"I was the class secretary," she said softly. "Did I ever tell you girls that?"

"Did Dad know about Peter?" Sharla asked.

I nodded. Good work.

"Oh, no. That was before I met your father. I had one more boyfriend before I met your father and that was

Frank Peabody. Best-tempered man I ever met. And the blackest hair."

"*PEABODY?*" I asked, forgetting our mission. I could have been Ginny *Pea*body! Under the table, Sharla kicked me.

I kicked her back.

"What are you *doing?*" my mother asked. She lifted the tablecloth, peered beneath it.

Exasperated, Sharla said, "Mom. Did you ever meet any of Dad's girlfriends?"

But it was too late, my mother was back in the unromantic present. "If you two want to fight, you can go right upstairs and do it. I do not want to be in the middle of it. In fact, since you have so much energy to waste, you can scour the bathroom sink and tub. Yes, you go on and do that—you can just help me with some of this housework. I'm pretty tired of doing so much of it myself."

A moment of frustrated silence and then, "Sink!" Sharla muttered, calling for the easier of the two jobs.

I made sure she didn't really win. I let her go first; then I shut the bathroom door, and let the tap run furiously as I sat on the edge of the tub and looked at *Reader's Digest*. I liked the jokes and the true-life stories that made you cry a little. I understood the attraction to a certain type of grief.

After I read for a while, I turned off the water. The tub looked perfectly clean, as it always did. My mother came in to inspect Sharla's and my work and nodded her approval. I had a moment of feeling guilty, but then reasoned that if the tub ever really did need cleaning, I would do it. There was no point in scrubbing away at something you couldn't even see. I longed for streaks of mud, for soap stuck in a sticky puddle at the bottom of the tub, even for the sickening thrill of blood, courtesy of my mother's injuring herself while shaving her legs. I wanted the satisfaction of seeing something change before my eyes, not the humdrum necessity of maintaining the status quo.

Now, boredom settling around me like dusk, I rose and went to our bedroom window, lifted my blouse to let the fan blow on me. Nothing doing outside, either. Not even a breeze. "Well, that's it, I'm going to get her," I said.

"You can't."

"Why not?"

"Because. She probably doesn't want to get interrupted. Just like when she goes to coffee klatch." Coffee klatch was the weekly gathering of the neighborhood ladies on the block, held in a different kitchen each week. I was excited about it being in our house until I heard what the women talked about: Detergent. Children. Their husbands' jobs. The coupons they exchanged with each other. No secrets were revealed; no one even laughed. Frankly, I saw no point in those meetings, except for perhaps the food. Mrs. Gooch brought a blueberry coffee cake to our house that was outstanding—Sharla and I fought over the buttery crumbs. The good thing about coffee klatch was that it lasted only an hour, and therefore we were not driven to feelings of desperation. But this!

"She's been there all *day*!" I told Sharla.

"Oh, stop whining. You don't know how long she's been there."

"More than two hours. Way more than that."

"That's not all day."

"Well, I'm going."

"Wait," Sharla said. "I'm coming."

Just as we were about to knock, Jasmine's door opened, and my mother came out, smiling. "Oh," she said. "Are you up?"

"It's *late*," I said.

"What time is it?"

"Almost *two*."

Jasmine appeared behind my mother. "It's one-fifteen," she said, looking at her watch. "Well. What are you two doing today?"

"Nothing," I said, moodily.

"I was just going over to Monroe's," Jasmine said. "Would you like to come?"

I looked at Sharla, who was nodding, then at my mother.

"You can go," she said.

The day had just flipped. A ride in Jasmine's red-and-white Chevy convertible to an air-conditioned store. Possibly a stop for an A&W on the way home; I'd never met anyone yet who didn't like A&W, and I intended to suggest it in an irresistibly casual way.

"You want to come, Marion?" Jasmine asked.

"No, thanks," my mother said. "It's much later than I thought. I've got to think about what to make for dinner."

"Oh, just have sandwiches," Jasmine said. "They don't take long to make."

Boy, I thought. She doesn't know my mother. She had to make a big dinner every night, even in the summer. But

I waited with some uneasiness until I heard my mother sigh and say that very thing.

Now, sitting here on this airplane, I stare at the seat pocket in front of me. There are the magazines I bought for the trip. *Bon Appétit. Gourmet. Cooks Illustrated.* And *The Atlantic Monthly*, of course, proving that I am nothing like her.

"Hot, huh?" Jasmine asked, as we backed slowly out of her driveway. I was watching her in the rearview mirror. She had on black wraparound sunglasses that were serious about their job—you couldn't see her eyes at all. She wore a silky leopard-print scarf over her hair and tied at the back of her neck, a sleeveless black dress and black sandals that were barely there—the straps seemed thin as rubber bands. Gold bangle bracelets clicked brightly on her arm. Sharla got to hold her black straw purse and I could tell she was pretending it was her own. Jasmine was like a deluxe, 3-D paper doll; she had clothes and accessories for every occasion. It was a pleasure to live next door to her, to see what she would be wearing each day. So far some of the things we had liked best were turquoise capri pants, bright yellow short shorts, gold earrings in the shape of seashells, and a two-piece navy-blue suit trimmed with white piping. We were dying to see her pajamas, but she closed her bedroom curtains at night before she undressed. Shortly after moving in, she had stretched out in a chaise longue in her backyard in a white bikini. I had never seen one outside of the *Life* magazine issue highlighting the French Riviera. Even my mother looked out the window for that outfit. For a while no one said anything; then my mother said, "Well, for heaven's sake, she's *already* tan, isn't she?" And then, sighing, "Hasn't she found a job yet?"

Jasmine signaled for a left. "What do you say we take a spin on the highway first? We'll open her up and cool off a little."

I settled happily into a corner of the backseat. I had an idea of how I would look with my hair blowing straight out, sitting in a convertible. Older.

Soon we were on the highway in the passing lane, and I saw the red needle of the speedometer trembling at the ninety-miles-an-hour mark. When I heard the wail of the siren behind us, I turned around to see a black-and-white police car far away, but closing in. "Uh-oh," I said. When I turned back I saw Jasmine looking into the rearview mirror and smiling. She reached over and put a hand on Sharla's knee, yelled, "Hold on!" and sped up.

I couldn't believe it. I laughed out loud, but I was very much afraid. It might be Leroy, for one thing; and then, even if Jasmine got away from him, he would know where to come—with the top down, he would have seen Sharla and me clearly. He would knock on our door, ask our mother where we were, and she would start wringing her hands. After we were standing straight before him, he would say something like, "Enjoy your little ride this afternoon? Care to tell me who the driver was?"

"Tell him!" my mother would say, her voice a mix of outrage and anguish. And then, "Oh, my goodness! It was Jasmine Johnson, wasn't it?" Actually, that would be fine; then she would be the tattletale.

Jasmine was in the right-hand lane now, going even faster. And then we were on an exit ramp, headed down a side street, then another and another. Finally she pulled into a Henny Penny, screeched to a halt, and turned off the ignition. The police car was nowhere in sight. "Everybody all right?" she asked.

Well. Sharla and I looked at each other. Sharla was still holding on to the door handle. I'd neglected to do that, and had slid from one end of the long backseat to the other.

"You okay?" Jasmine asked again.

"Yes, ma'am," Sharla said. I nodded.

Jasmine looked into the mirror, adjusted her scarf and her glasses. "I hate when they do that," she said. "Chase you around like you're a common criminal." She pressed her lips together, touched lightly at a corner of her mouth. Then she turned back to me, lowered her sunglasses. "What's the matter, honey?"

"Nothing."

"Do you want to go home?"

"No, ma'am."

"So . . . shall we continue? Monroe's?"

I nodded.

She turned to my sister. "Sharla?"

"What?"

"Monroe's?"

"Okay."

Her voice was small. It came to me that she wasn't so old.

Jasmine took her purse from Sharla, pulled out a package of Lucky Strikes. "Damn," she said. "Only one left. I'm going to run in the store for a second. You want to come?"

I shook my head; I wasn't sure I trusted my knees yet. But Sharla went with her and when they came out she was eating a Baby Ruth. I was annoyed until Jasmine handed a Milky Way to me.

"Thank you," I said. "Did Sharla tell you this is my favorite?"

"No, I guessed. You're a Milky Way type, don't you think?"

I unwrapped the candy bar, shrugged. I was all of a sudden in a bad mood. I didn't want to be so easy.

I liked Monroe's department store. It was big, but not intimidating, and carried enough merchandise to always be interesting. It had wooden floors and high ceilings with intricate engravings, white on white. I used to lie on my back to admire the ceiling whenever my mother wasn't looking, until the day I was stepped on by Mrs. Reginald Whalen, the principal's wife, who apologized profusely to my mother for the dirty mark she left behind on my white blouse. I myself feared (and hoped) that my ribs had been broken, and felt around gingerly while my mother held me to her and nervously reassured Mrs. Whalen that no, a visit to the emergency room would not be necessary. Alas, I was not even bruised, and after my mother mildly chastised me for nearly tripping such an important person, we finished our shopping without incident.

Sharla liked the department stores in the big cities that we visited at Christmastime, but I felt mostly in the way there, out of place. I didn't think a choice of fifteen or twenty winter coats was necessary; at Monroe's, there might be a choice of three, which felt exactly right to me. And there were no mysterious bonging bells there, no glitzy counters staffed by impatient young women wearing too much makeup. There were no escalators; if you wanted to go upstairs to the second or third floor, you simply walked. There were large departments for men's clothing, women's clothing, juniors, and children's; and there were smaller sections for many other things. Cardboard rounds of satin ribbons were lined up on wooden dowels in the stationery department; soft linen handkerchiefs featuring pastel embroidery overlapped each other in glass display cases in Notions—the woman who usually worked in that department had a whispery voice like a librarian, and she sucked continually, though inoffensively, on hard candies. Nylon stockings were stacked high in their thin blue boxes along the side wall in Hosiery, and this department was always busy. Women waiting their turns chatted softly with each other, rested their pocketbooks on the counter, removed one foot from a high-heeled shoe to rub the top of the other. The jewelry department featured a small selection of watches, necklaces, and bracelets that, despite their sparkly allure, did not need to be locked up.

There was a fairly large hat department toward the front of the store, and this is where Jasmine headed first. She tried on every hat displayed, and encouraged us to do the same. Sharla did, but I stopped after three; the hats looked too silly on me and too perfect on Jasmine. I liked watching her in the mirror more than looking at myself. She lifted her chin, turned her head this way and that when she tried on one flamboyant offering. It had a huge white brim with a dip over one eye; I thought she would buy it, and she did. She offered to buy Sharla a hat as well, a small black cloche, but Sharla declined with a mixture of propriety and regret.

We went next to Intimates, and Jasmine disappeared into a dressing room with an armload of brassieres, panties, and slips. She had told Sharla and me to pick out something for ourselves, but we were uninspired to do anything but rifle through the nightgowns, looking to see if one might work for my mother's birthday, which was exactly two weeks before my own. I did not want to give my mother a nightgown; I thought the idea lacked imagination. However, my offering last year had been licorice and a book of riddles, which I now saw differently.

"Girls," Jasmine called, her head sticking out from her dressing room. "Could you get me another size in a slip? The one I have in here is way too big."

I looked around for the sales clerk, but she was busy helping someone else with girdles. "What do you need?" I asked, coming up to the curtain.

"One minute, let me get this off," Jasmine said, turning to remove the slip she had on. She did not close the curtain all the way back up, and I watched her standing there in a bra, panties, and nylons. She looked like the lingerie models in the Sears catalogue that I studied behind the closed bathroom door; but her figure was more spectacular, and disturbingly real. There was a small constellation of moles on one side of her back; her belly button was slightly elongated; the line of her tan stopped dramatically above soft-looking white breasts. She looked up, saw me watching, and smiled. I shut the curtain. When her hand came out holding the slip, I walked away quickly, blushing.

"What's wrong with you?" Sharla asked.

"Nothing." I handed the slip to her, told her to find a

smaller size and bring it to Jasmine, that I was going over to look at toys for a minute.

"Well, hurry up," Sharla said, but it wasn't really me she was talking to. And it wasn't really toys I was going over to consider.

Jasmine bought hula hoops for Sharla and me; Monroe's had just gotten them in. And after we got home, Sharla and I spent a long time in the backyard learning how to use them. I was surprised to find that I was at last better at something than Sharla—and so was she. I got the hoop going around my waist almost right away, but Sharla's kept falling down. After a short while, I could walk around with it spinning evenly, while Sharla had abandoned her waist and was trying to twirl the hoop on her arm. I thought this might be even harder; but Sharla was frustrated and in no mood for tips from me.

Gypsy, Jasmine's German shepherd, lay nearby. I took a break to allow Sharla time to catch up, and stretched out close beside the dog. I liked watching the slick black sides of her mouth move back and forth with her panting. Occasionally, a fly would hover around her and she would snap at it. I liked that, too. And if you scratched in the right place, her back leg would react wildly, while her dog face remained utterly impassive. I very much wanted a dog, but my mother would not permit it. Not a dog, not a cat; only a parakeet, which she said she could keep track of. I knew what she meant. A parakeet couldn't mess up the house. It was the one thing I truly hated about my mother, her devotion to an orderly house. I couldn't imagine why it meant so much to her. It seemed to me that she could risk a little messiness in her life in order to gain real pleasure. But she always said, "You let one thing slip, and it all goes."

Once, I called my mother outside to watch Gypsy as she ate potato chips, but my mother was not persuaded to my point of view. "She's drooling," my mother said, and I said, "No, listen to the *crunch*!" She listened dutifully, then smiled blankly and went back inside.

Jasmine had called my mother over to show off her purchases when we returned from shopping, and though my mother protested that she was in the middle of making dinner and couldn't leave, she went anyway. At one point, I saw through Jasmine's dining-room window that my mother was wearing the new white hat. I stopped twirling my hula hoop. "Look," I told Sharla. I pointed to the window.

Sharla looked, then turned away, scowling. "*She* doesn't wear hats like that," she said. I supposed I agreed, but I kept watching my mother until she took the hat off and laid it on the table before her. She had looked beautiful in it. And starkly unlike herself. Watching her, I'd felt the way that babies seemed to feel regarding themselves in a mirror: ah! Look! Something lovable, and familiar, and intriguing. But entirely separate.

I take out my credit card, use the plane phone to call home. No one answers, and I don't leave a message. I just wanted anyone who was there to know I was there, too, in a way. Only a phone call away. Even in the air. Oftentimes I sense a polite impatience when I am on a rare trip and I call my daughters. But I have to let them know something.

A couple of years ago my husband and I took a brief trip to Canada. When I called home for the third time one day, my husband exploded. "Why must you do this?" he asked. "What do you think *happened*? They're fine!"

"I know that!" I said. "I just want them to know we're thinking of them."

"They're *fine*," he said again, and I sniffed, looked out the hotel window, and sulked for a few minutes. I knew I was overdoing it, yet I felt compelled to make those calls. It had to do with the way parents say they'll never repeat the mistakes their own parents made. It had to do with my offering my daughters what I so needed and was denied. I couldn't imagine why they wouldn't be grateful. How could they not be grateful when surely they could see that I was only trying to love them, to give them what I knew they needed—whether they knew it or not?

73

And now some wave of feeling comes over me that I don't recognize. Nausea? I sit still for a moment, then rise quickly and head back to the lavatory, which thankfully is free. Inside, I kneel before the stainless-steel toilet, hold back my hair, and wait. Nothing. I wash my face, rinse out my mouth, and stare at myself in the dimly lit mirror. I don't look sick. I don't feel sick anymore, either. I shrug, head back to my seat, settle in, and continue with my memories the way I might keep on with a book.

When my mother returned home from trying on Jasmine's hat, she was flushed and happy. Through the open kitchen window I heard her humming with the radio. "Catch a Falling Star" was playing. I liked that song, too, liked the notion of having a pocketful of starlight. I hoped for such a thing, in fact. I believed at the time that stars were five-pointed objects you could hold in your hand, a sort of fancier version of the tinfoil variety. I was ignorant of heat and size and the most astounding fact of all, that some stars I saw were not really there at all. I counted on someday finding a falling star and I had resolved not to share it with Sharla, no matter how convincing her arguments might be. She could *look* at it as it lay on my bed; that was all.

"Hula hoops are stupid," Sharla finally said, after failing yet again to keep hers up. She threw it down, headed for the woods.

"Nuh-uh," I said, walking jerkily, following her, my hula hoop going around my waist in a way that felt like a sloppy embrace. "They're *fun*."

"Well, something is wrong with mine," Sharla said. "It doesn't work."

I put my hot-pink hula hoop down, picked up her

lime-green one, started spinning it. "It works," I called out. "Hey, Sharla, look! It works!"

She would not turn around.

"You're just a party pooper!" I called after her. And then I attempted to spin both hoops at the same time, but failed. I stepped out of them to follow Sharla.

"Someone has ravaged our lands," Sharla said. "We must have a war dance." Sharla was excellent at war dances. My job was to watch her, to sit cross-legged at the circle of rocks we called a campfire, and make rhythmic, singing sounds, while Sharla twirled and whirled, bent down low and raised up high, calling for power from heaven and earth.

When we ate dinner the next Monday night, my vocabulary word was "sanguine." "He has a sanguine disposition," I told the table. "He thinks everything will always be fine."

"Well . . . all right," my father said, and then turned expectantly toward Sharla.

"Seductive," she said. "She is very seductive."

No one spoke. I knew the word Sharla had chosen wasn't far in the dictionary from the one I had picked. She sometimes deliberated for a long time before choosing her word, but tonight she had merely flipped a few pages away, closed her eyes, and pointed.

"I don't get what it means," I said now, spearing a green bean.

"She is s*educt*ive," Sharla said. "She tries to be *sex*y like Brigitte Bardot. You know. Va-va-va-*voom*!"

"That's fine," my mother said. "We understand."

"Or," Sharla persisted. "She *is* seductive; she tries to *cap*ture things."

"Enough," my father said, and looked over his fork at my mother, who looked away.

After dinner, while Sharla and I did the dishes, we heard my mother talking to my father in the living room. "How would you define happiness?" she asked him.

Sharla and I looked at each other.

". . . What are you talking about?" my father said.

"It's just a question, Steven."

"Well, I don't know what you mean."

"I mean . . . well, I guess I mean just what I said! You know? How would you define happiness? What *is* it? Is it real? And if it is, what brings it to you? Is it something in you or outside of you? Does anyone have it all the time, or are there just moments of happiness for anyone? Is contentment the same as happiness?"

Silence. And then my father said, "Good Lord. What have you been reading, Marion?"

She sighed. "Steven, I just wanted to . . . oh, forget it. All right? Forget it."

Silence again, and then the television came on. I snuck out into the hall to peek into the living room. I wanted to make sure they were sitting beside each other on the sofa, that my mother had not retreated to her knitting chair, where she went when she was angry. Her needles flew then, clicked brightly, speaking a language only she could understand.

She was on the sofa beside my father. And his arm was around her, his usual loose claim. But while he was watching *The Rifleman*, she was watching her hands in her lap. They didn't move. I couldn't imagine what she was seeing.

"They're okay," I told Sharla doubtfully, when I came back into the kitchen.

"*I* know," she said irritably, and in her anger was the same fear I felt.

Sharla and I slept in our beds that night. It felt odd, not being outside on our quilt first. At one point, I woke up, full of resentment at my mother for having discovered us and taken away this simple pleasure. "Sharla?" I whispered.

She was sleeping. I looked at our clock. Two-ten.

"Sharla!"

"*What?*"

"Want to sneak out?"

"We can't."

"Why not?"

"They said not to, we'll get in trouble."

"They won't catch us, they're asleep."

"How do you know?"

"They're always asleep by now. They're always asleep a long time ago."

Sharla turned on her side, away from me. "You check. If they're sound asleep, maybe."

I got out of bed. I'd go to the bathroom first. If the flushing toilet didn't wake them, our creeping downstairs surely wouldn't. I wanted to do something more tonight. I wanted to take a walk somewhere we'd never been.

I turned on the bathroom light and there was my mother, sitting on the edge of the bathtub. Her feet were bare, her nightgown pulled up over her knees. She looked at me, squinting in the light, said nothing.

"Mom! What are you *doing*?" I said. I was angry; she'd scared me.

"Well, I . . ." She seemed a bit angry herself. Her cheeks were pink, her breathing rapid. "As you can see, I'm sitting here."

"How come?"

She rose, squeezed past me. "Not everything I do is your business." She looked at herself in the mirror, pushed the sides of her hair back. Then she left.

I stood for a moment, stunned. Why was she behaving this way? I hadn't done anything, had I? No. I flushed the toilet, turned the faucet on and off, and went back to the bedroom.

Sharla was asleep again, and I didn't wake her. I lay in bed for a while, then went to see if Jasmine's bedroom light was on. No. And yet I believed I could feel her wakefulness.

I wonder now if my mother didn't owe it to me to say something at that point. To say *something* about what she must have been thinking. Or feeling. Or planning.

I had a friend who got leukemia and for the longest time would not tell her seven- and nine-year-old sons. In the interest of protecting them, she tried to pretend that her frequent doctor's visits were outings with friends, shopping trips, appointments with the dentist. At the point when she was losing all her hair and she finally had to tell them, they said they had thought she was tired of them. This is a woman who sat immobilized at the kitchen table holding her older son's pajamas on the day he first went to nursery school, willing him to be safe on the bus, in the classroom, on the monkey bars, at snack time.

If there is a fault I, too, have as a parent, it is over-protectiveness, I know. But I'll tell you this: my children know they can depend on me to tell them the truth. If ever something started happening in me the way it did in my mother, I'd tell my children. I'd tell them *some*thing.

One morning I awakened to the sound of thunder and pelting rain. I pulled the sheet up higher, then reached for the bedspread to cover me. It felt good to wake up chilly after so many hot nights. I saw that the fan had been turned off and the window closed; I shut my eyes to feel better the head-to-toe pleasure of having been cared for in my sleep. The thunder came again, a sound so loud it made the whole house seem to shake.

"Sharla?" I said.

No response. She couldn't be sleeping! I called her name again; again I heard no response. I got out of bed, peered down at her. I noticed no give-away eye movements, no secret smile, only the no-access blankness of a face deep in sleep.

I stretched, put on socks and my robe and headed downstairs for breakfast. I wanted French toast; I was visualizing a fat pat of butter melting over two perfect slices, warmed syrup being poured over that.

My mother was sitting at the kitchen table, poring over her "house folder," as she called it. In this she kept magazine photographs of furniture she could not afford, swatches of fabric she could never use, and layouts for gardens both small and grand, though we never had a garden. The file also held graph paper for planning furniture rearrangements; and this was a passion my mother realized. She made scaled-down paper cutouts representing every piece of furniture we had, taped the edges for durability, and moved them around on the graph paper until she was satisfied; then she duplicated her efforts for real. You never knew when she would strike. You would come home from school and find her standing in the middle of a new living room, her finger to her chin, musing, making sure she was really done.

I was astounded at how my mother was able to move furniture alone—sometimes I'd find the heavy sofa on the other side of the room, the china cabinet in the dining room reoriented in order to maximize the afternoon light falling onto the cut-crystal glasses.

"Who helped you?" I would ask every time; and every time she would shrug and say, "No one." I often imagined her in a phone booth, changing into some Superwoman costume in order to achieve such things, but she wore only a cleaning kerchief and dungarees (neatly belted, of course, with a nicely ironed blouse tucked into them). I would try out the new arrangement: lie on the sofa, read in a chair, turn on the television in its new place. I liked feeling as though I'd moved without having had to go anywhere; it gave me a safe thrill. Sharla and my father complained that it made them feel mixed up, that there was no reason to do such things; there was never anything wrong with the way things *were*.

My mother compromised by never changing around anything upstairs—the placement of things in her and my father's bedroom, especially, was sacrosanct. I once used my mother's hairbrush when I was in her room talking to her as she folded laundry on the bed. When I put the brush down on the left side of her dresser, she actually stopped what she was doing to come over and move it to the right. It was not cruel in any way, or even particularly admonitory; it was just that up here, things *stayed*. There was a pleasurable aspect to that, I supposed, but it confused me, too. Why, in that room only, did there have to be such a sense of change as sin?

On the rainy morning I found my mother staring at her magazine pictures, I thought it might be another redecorating day. Hard to say for sure, though; the cleaning kerchief was nowhere in sight—my mother was still in her robe. This surprised me; it was almost eleven.

I sat at the table across from her. "What are you doing?"

She looked up. "What?"

I pointed to the pictures. "What are you doing?"

"Oh," she said, closing the folder, "nothing, really. Looking. Dreaming."

"Dreaming of what?"

"Oh, of how I'd *really* like things." She smiled, raised her eyebrows. "You know, I wish—"

"Can I have some French toast?" I asked. I hadn't meant to interrupt, but I was hungry; and I was afraid if she started telling me what she'd really like, breakfast would be delayed for a good long while.

Her smile changed, and she rose to open the refrigerator. When she was beating the milk into the eggs, I said, "So . . . what do you wish?"

"Never mind." Her voice was quiet, flat. She didn't look up. She served me perfectly browned French toast, kissed the top of my head, then went upstairs to dress. I ate alone, stared out the window at the rain. I saw that Sharla's and my latest tepee, made out of branches tied together with twine, had collapsed. There'd be no repairing anything today, though. Today would be an indoor day: Parcheesi. Monopoly, the money limp and folding over in our hands from the humidity. Store, with Sharla hogging the role of cashier. Crazy 8s, Go Fish, War. Dishes would pile up in the sink from our frequent snacks, eating being the favorite recreation of the trapped. Already I was thinking of S'mores, of how I might convince my mother that they were fine to have before lunch. Or for lunch, for that matter.

Sharla came to the table when I had just finished eating. "What did you have?" she asked.

"French toast. It was good. There's more; it's on the plate by the stove."

"I don't want French toast. I hate French toast."

"You do not."

"Do so."

"No you do not. You ate it last week!"

"So? You can change what you like."

My mother entered the kitchen. "If you girls want to fight," she said, "go outside." There was a thinness in her voice that I had never heard before, a tautness.

"It's _rain_ing," Sharla said.

"I could not care less."

Sharla and I looked at each other, silently agreeing to abandon our fighting for the sake of this much more interesting turn of events.

"We would catch pneumonia," Sharla said.

My mother wet the dishrag, began wiping off the counter. "I suppose you could."

"We could die," I said playfully.

She looked up at me, shrugged. "There are worse things."

"What do you *mean*?" I asked.

She didn't answer. The blank passivity in her face reminded me of watching Sharla sleep. Then she looked down at the counter, wiped and wiped in circles, at nothing.

"Mom?" She was scaring me; I wanted to grab the dishrag away from her and throw it on the floor. I wanted to kick her.

She stopped wiping, looked wearily up at me. "Oh, Ginny, *what*?" There. She was back. Somewhat. At least she was looking at me. "What do you want?"

"Well, *I* want pancakes," Sharla said.

"You don't want French toast?" my mother asked.

"I hate French toast."

"Fine." She dumped the leftover French toast in the garbage, cracked an egg against the side of a bowl for pancakes. In my mind, the sound rivaled the thunder. No one spoke. We watched our mother make pancakes, but cautiously, the way the hunter parts the grass to observe the wild beast.

"What's wrong with *her*?" Sharla asked, after our mother had set pancakes in front of her and once again left the room.

I shrugged.

She took a big swallow of orange juice, then said, "*I* know what's wrong."

"So why did you ask me?"

"I wanted to see if you knew, too."

"Maybe I do."

"Maybe you don't." Sharla cut her pancakes into neat squares. She always cut her food this way, and it annoyed and fascinated me both. I rested my chin on my folded arms, watching her.

"Stop," Sharla said.

"What?"

"Stop watching me."

"I'm not watching you, I'm watching your fork."

"Well, stop."

She loaded up a fork with pancake squares, shoved them into her mouth, then spoke around them. "She misses Jasmine," she said.

"Who does?"

"Mom!"

"Where's Jasmine?"

"She's out of town. She went to Mobile, Alabama."

"What for?"

"I don't know. I just know she went. Because I wanted to go visit her yesterday and Mom said, 'She just left,' and it was all sad-like."

"How long's she gone for?"

"A week. Six more days."

I considered this. Then, "Want to snoop over there?" I asked. We had a key to Jasmine's house. She and my mother had exchanged keys only a few days after Jasmine moved in.

Sharla did not answer. I took this as a good sign.

"Tonight, midnight?" I asked, and again she did not answer.

Well, then. Plans cast in stone.

*   *   *

When I went upstairs to dress, I saw my parents' bedroom door open. The bedside lamp was on; the sky had
darkened considerably. I saw the rain pounding sideways
at the window, as if seeking furious entry. My mother
was lying on her unmade bed. She was on her back, one
arm resting across her closed eyes. Her ankles were crossed
neatly, shoes lined up at the side of the bed.

"Mom?" I whispered.

"Yes?" She did not take her arm away or open her eyes.

"Are you sick?"

Now she did open her eyes. Then she sat up and stared
at me for some time before she answered.

"Yes," she finally said, softly. And then, louder, "Yes. I
have . . . a headache."

"Want us to do anything?"

"Don't fight."

"Okay." I closed her door, then went back into Sharla's
and my bedroom. I made both our beds, put our dirty
clothes in the laundry hamper, wadded up a bunch of
toilet tissue to dust the furniture and along the window
ledge. I was sorry for everything, because I didn't know
what specifically to be sorry for. But I felt the weight of
regret spread wide across my chest. This always happened when my mother got sick. I was sorry, I was sorry,
I was sorry.

I've talked some with other mothers about what we
learned from our own. Here's something I learned: I
never make my children think any illness I have has anything to do with them. I never do that. Never. I mean, for
God's sake.

At midnight, Sharla and I crossed quietly through our damp backyard and over into Jasmine's. We crept around the side of her house opposite our own and then Sharla unlocked the heavy front door. I was having a little trouble waking up, which disappointed me; I'd wanted to feel nervous, or at least guilty. But the truth is, we had seen every room in Jasmine's house; there was nothing for us to discover unless we went rifling through her private belongings, and I wasn't sure I was ready for that. Sharla was, though; she went directly to Jasmine's bedroom and opened a large dresser drawer. The beam of my flashlight focused on pastel-colored, silky things. I saw a number of straps, a lot of lace. This whole drawer was underwear?

"What are you looking for?" I asked.

"Anything," Sharla said; and then, turning accusingly toward me, she added, "This was your stupid idea."

"Nuh-uh, I didn't say to do this part." I looked more closely at the contents of the drawer. Yes, all underwear; there was the slip she'd gotten at Monroe's. I wondered whether anything was hidden beneath the underwear; I myself once drew a picture of a naked woman with huge breasts and kept it hidden in my underwear drawer. I removed it after only a few hours, though—tore it into many pieces and flushed it down the toilet.

"We shouldn't look in her personal stuff," I said, hoping Sharla would ignore me.

She took the flashlight from me and shone it into my face; I held up my hand, squinted at her through my fingers. "What do *you* want to do," she asked, in her most irritating big-sister voice, "get a drink of water out of her kitchen sink or something? Go pee in her toilet?"

I said nothing, waiting for what I thought was misplaced anger to dissipate. Then I said, "We could try on her fur coats. I know exactly where they are."

"Big deal, so do I. Anyway, she'd let us do that anytime we wanted."

True. Jasmine was open and generous, more so than anyone we'd ever met. You had to be careful about saying you liked something she had; she'd up and give it to you. And then you'd get in trouble with our mother; so far, I'd had to return two scarves, a pair of pearl earrings, and the current issue of *The Saturday Evening Post*, although my mother said that when the new issue came out, I could have that old one.

Sharla pulled out a picture frame from the underwear drawer, shone the flashlight on it. It was a photograph of a boy, a teenager. He was brown-haired, blue-eyed, and very handsome, sitting on the steps of a huge porch and smiling. The fingers of his hands were loosely linked between his knees, his feet were bare. He wore blue jeans and a white T-shirt. Beside him, a cat lay sleeping.

"Who's that?" I asked.

"How should I know?" Sharla shoved the picture back into the drawer, opened another. Behind a stack of neatly folded nightgowns, she found something that made her gasp. She pulled out a yellow cellophane package, a small square.

"What is it?" I asked. Ah. I was awake. I felt as though shards of sleep were dropping around me like eggshell around a hatching bird.

"Don't look!" She started to shove the thing back into the drawer.

I grabbed it from her, held it up to have a look. "A balloon?"

"It is *not* a bal*loon*." Sharla took the thing from me, put it back in the drawer. "Let's go downstairs. I'll tell you what it is."

Sharla instructed me to sit on one end of the sofa, and she sat on the other. "Now," she said, hands folded in her lap, legs crossed. She was speaking in the voice she used for playing teacher. I regretted the fact that she was not wearing a pair of high heels; everything worked better then. She leaned toward me, spoke quietly. "What exactly do you know about s-e-x?"

"Just where babies come from."

"You *do* know that?"

"Yes. They come out of the mother's belly button."

Sharla stared at me, smiled. "Very well," she said. "But how do the babies *get* in the mother's stomach?"

"The fathers do it."

"How?"

"I haven't gotten that far."

"All right. It's time for you to know."

I sat up straighter. I loved Sharla.

"The man has a penis, you know that, right?"

"A wiener."

"It is called a penis."

"A *boinger*," I said, and laughed loudly.

"Well, Ginny, do you want to learn something or do you just want to fool around?"

I made my expression instantly serious. "I want to learn."

"Fine. Then be quiet, and listen to me. The man has a penis which he puts inside the woman and sprays things out. The things are called semen. And that is seed that makes the baby grow."

"Oh."

"You have a hole in you for where the semens go."

"I don't think I have it yet," I said. I inspected myself to the best of my ability with some regularity.

"Yes, you do; you are born with it, every girl baby is born right with it attached."

"Oh."

"Now. If a woman does not want semens in her, she makes the man wear a rubber. And that is what is in Jasmine's drawer right now. A *pile* of them."

"For what?" I was incredulous.

"What do you think? For when she has sex with men!" Sharla uncrossed her hands and her legs, fell out of her role.

"She doesn't do that!"

"How do you know? You don't know."

"I have never seen one man at her house," I said. I was absolutely sure of this.

"You are not with her all the time, are you? Anyway, she probably goes over to their houses. There are bachelor pads. They have round beds, and they have music that comes out of the wall."

"But she has the rubbers *here*."

"She *puts* one in her *purse*," Sharla said.

I stopped breathing. I'd eaten gum from that purse.

"Oh yes," Sharla said. "She has sex, all right. I'm not a bit surprised."

"Me neither," I said. But I was.

"I want to see it again," I said.

"The rubber?"

"Yes."

She sighed. "Oh, all *right*." She wanted to see it again too, obviously.

We went back to Jasmine's bedroom. Sharla pulled out one of the rubbers, held it aloft between two fingers. I stared at it. It had a definite presence. I nearly expected it to introduce itself.

"Want to hold it?" Sharla asked.

I took the rubber from her, put it in the palm of my hand, pressed down on it gingerly. The hard, rolled edge of the thing made for an unpleasant little chill that rose up along my neck. My knees felt watery.

"She has about six million of them," Sharla said. "Look." I looked. There was indeed a pile of them, at least ten.

I put the rubber up next to my crotch. "Look, I'm the man." I swayed my pelvis slowly back and forth. "Hey, baby, give me a smooch. Kiss me; kiss me, baby." I closed my eyes, made wet smacking sounds, then began gyrating wildly. I had done this before, with the vacuum hose held to my crotch—but only alone.

"Don't make me puke," Sharla said.

I opened my eyes, handed her the rubber. "Here."

"You put it back. I don't want to touch it anymore."

"Maybe I'll keep it," I said.

"Ha."

I put the rubber in my robe pocket.

"Wait till Mom finds *that*," Sharla said.

"She won't."

"Where will you hide it that she won't know?"

"Same place I hide things that *you* don't know about," I said smugly.

"You don't have a place like that."

"Do, too." It was an old jewelry box I kept in the back of our closet. I put it there soon after I had torn up my naked-woman drawing. I positioned a toothpick strategically up against the side of the box so that I would know if anyone went near it. So far, no one had. Inside the box were pictures from magazines of kissing couples, a ring I found on the classroom floor last year and did not report finding, and a silver dollar from Uncle Roy. Also a nylon stocking I'd found in the trash and liked to put on when no one was home.

"I have a hiding place, too," Sharla said.

"I doubt it."

"Doubt it, then; I do."

"So? I don't care." And I didn't care, exactly, but I was a little hurt. Surprised that I had not known this. Where was her place? I wondered. And then it came to me that probably everyone had a place. Everyone.

Sharla and I left Jasmine's house different people. It seemed to me we were simultaneously disappointed in and more respectful of each other—such was the mixed effect of unearthing long-held secrets.

I heard the cellophane package in my pocket making

small noises all the way home. When we got to our bedroom, I put the rubber under my mattress—it would stay there until I could be alone to hide it. I had no idea why I wanted it. It made me feel sick. But there was a thrill to the sickness, a jazzy edge that made what felt like an internal eyeball jerk open. Therefore it was worth it.

I closed my eyes, settled in for sleep. An image came to me: Jasmine's face, her red mouth smiling. She was looking away from me; then she looked right at me, and she knew everything. Everything. She kept smiling. I felt an enormous sense of relief. Then guilt.

Sharla woke me up a few nights later calling my name. "What do you want?" I asked, my voice croaky, my mouth stuck to itself. I tried to open my eyes, but I was dizzy with fatigue, and so I shut them again. I hoped Sharla wasn't sick; I didn't feel like helping her.

"What are you *do*ing?" she asked.

I remained silent; the answer was obvious.

"Ginny?" she whispered.

"What?" I whispered back.

"Are you awake now?"

"*Yes,* I'm *talk*ing to you." I was not whispering any longer.

"Well, I have to be sure. You could be talking in your sleep, you know."

"You don't have conversations in your sleep!"

"Yes you do. I learned it in science that you can have an actual conversation and yet still be sleeping. Mr. Weaver told us."

I considered this, yawned, scratched my knee. "Well, then how do we ever know the difference?" I asked.

"What do you mean?"

"Like, how do we know we're not asleep all the time?"

Sharla sighed loudly. "You don't *ever* stay on the real subject!"

"Well, what is the subject? You never even said. Plus why are you waking me up? I'm tired! It's late!"

"You never said that before, when we used to sneak out."

"Yes, because there was a *reason*, then, to wake up. Now you are just talking. And you aren't even making any sense."

The door opened, and our mother stood before us. "What's going on in here?" she asked. "What are you doing?"

"Sharla is going crazy, that's what, smack in the middle of the night." I flipped my pillow, punched it, flung myself back down onto it, sighed loudly.

"She's so stupid," Sharla said. "I woke her up to tell her one thing, and she starts a fight."

"I did not!" I sat up in bed, yanked my T-shirt strap up over my shoulder. I wished I were in pajamas, which were more dignified.

"Stop your yelling," my mother said. "You'll wake up your father."

"Did we wake you up?" I asked.

She sat down at the foot of Sharla's bed. "No. I was up."

I looked at our bedside clock: four-fifteen. I had a rush of misplaced excitement; this was like a sudden slumber party.

"How come you were up?" Sharla asked my mother.

"I was downstairs, reading."

"*Now?*" I strained to see her face. She was smiling, it appeared.

"Yes, now," she said. "It's nice, sometimes, to read in the middle of the night. The sky is so dark and soft-looking outside the window, all the stars out. You have just one light on, you know, and it seems to *pour* onto the page. Makes the book seem better. You are this little island, just up alone with a book. And you hear the night sounds of the house. You hear . . . water sounds, and things—well, turning on and off, I guess. You hear little creaks and groans, it's as though the whole house is sighing and moving in its sleep. Just like we do. And you know how we never notice the grandfather clock during the day? At night, you hear every little tick. It's so interesting to me, that sound. Time. The measure of it."

I lay still in my bed, eyes wide. I had never heard my mother go on in this way. I had never known she got up to read in the middle of the night. It was something I never would have done. Going out in the dark with Sharla was fine adventure; being in it alone terrified me, even in the confines of my own familiar bedroom. I believed that when you turned the lights out, cloaked figures materialized and lurked in the corners. They waited. They pointed at you with long, bony fingers, breathed long, ragged breaths, desired you with a terrible desire. I was safe so long as there was another person present, or a light; they would not touch me then. But to walk downstairs alone, voluntarily, in the dark!

My mother's voice sounded as though she were reading to us, as though she were present but also removed. She seemed peculiarly unavailable. I wanted to look at Sharla, to see what she thought about all this, but I was afraid if I moved my mother would stop talking. I was somewhat distressed by what she was saying, yet I wanted to hear more.

But then Sharla said, "I had a bad dream."

"Did you?" My mother turned toward her, yanked out of her reverie.

"Yes."

"What was it?" Her voice was low and level now, silky; her tone once again that of competent caretaker. Never mind the dream; no matter what it was, she would take it away.

"I dreamed . . ." Sharla said.

We waited.

"You had a third *eye*," she told my mother, and shuddered on "eye" as though she were swallowing something raw. "It was on the side of your head. It blinked and looked around and everything, all like a real eye."

"*I* had that?" my mother asked.

"Yes."

"Well," she said. "Was it pretty? Was it green? I always wanted green eyes. Did it wink at you?"

"This is not funny," Sharla said. "It was scary. You'd had it all along, and you never even told us. And then we were outside and your hair blew up and there was another *eye*ball in your head. It was scary!"

"I'm sorry," my mother said.

"It was a *dream*," I said. Why did she feel she needed to apologize?

"Well," my mother said, "you know what I mean. I'm sorry she had a bad dream." Then, to Sharla, "I don't have a third eye."

Sharla said nothing.

"You want to look?"

"No."

"Oh, come on," she said, and turned on the light, pulled her hair back. Then, "See? I'm just me."

Sharla yawned. "I know."

"All right then." My mother turned out the light. She pulled the sheet up over Sharla, kissed her forehead. "Go back to sleep."

She started out the door, then headed over to me, kissed my forehead, too. I smelled perfume on her; I had never smelled it on her late at night before. She said she was herself, but she wasn't. For instance, she smelled like Ivory soap at night, not perfume. Ivory soap.

After a few minutes, I said, ". . . Sharla?"

"What?" she whispered.

"Was that what you wanted to tell me, your dream?"

"Yes. But also that it was so *real*."

"I know," I said. And I believed I did. I turned onto my back, put my hands one over the other across my chest. Sometimes I liked to pretend I was dead.

As if somehow picking up on my thoughts, I hear the boy Glen's voice floating back to me. "If there's a crash," he says, "would we all die?"

Silence.

"Dad?"

"There won't be a crash," his father says quietly.

"Glen!" his sister says, not quietly. "You shouldn't try to hex us!"

"I'm not trying to hex us! I'm just asking. I can ask whatever I want. There is no such thing as a stupid question, stupid."

"That's only true sometimes," his sister says. "They just tell you that sometimes, when it's okay to ask anything right then."

"Well, now is okay, too. Isn't it, Dad?"

"Yes, it is, Glen," the father says, and I hear a certain tightening in his voice. He is getting ready.

"So, *would* we all die?"

"Well. As I said, there is not going to be a crash. But if there were, the truth is I don't know if anyone would die at all. Maybe there would just be some damage to the plane."

"But maybe also we *could* all die, right?"

I see the older couple across from me look at each other, smile ruefully.

Finally, "It's theoretically possible; yes," the father says.

"Told you," Glen says.

"Why don't we get another Coke?" his sister asks. "We can have all the Cokes we want, they have to give them to you whenever you ask."

Over Glen's seat, the call button goes on. Give me a Coke; I could be ready to die over here.

One night after dinner my father asked who wanted to go to Dairy Queen. This was a silly question; all of us always wanted to go to Dairy Queen. But not on this night. On this night, my mother said, "Why don't you all go ahead? I'm not much in the mood for ice cream." We all stared at her. "Well, I'm *sorry*," she said. "I just . . . I don't feel quite right."

"Is it—?" my father began, but she interrupted him, her hand over his, saying, "It's nothing, I'm sure. I just feel a little off. You go ahead, I'll stay here and watch television. I'll be fine." She stood up and began clearing the dishes.

"That's our job," I said. "We do that. You shouldn't do it if you're sick, anyway."

"I can clear the table," she said. "I just don't feel like eating ice cream."

"We'll bring you back a sundae; you can keep it in the freezer," my father said.

"That would be nice. Thank you." She smiled at him.

Something that had started tightening in my chest now relaxed. I went to change shorts; I wanted to wear the loosest waistband I had.

After we were out of sight of the house, my father

pulled the car over. "Who wants to help drive?" he asked.

"I do!" both Sharla and I said. I loved it when we got to do this, and it was rare. You had to be in the car with just my father—my mother wouldn't permit us to "drive"; and we were hardly ever in the car without her. What happened was, whoever was "helping" sat by my father and steered. He would take his hands off the wheel completely, saying, "I trust you, go ahead." And then, "I *trust* you, I trust you now. Okay. Okay." Finally he would shout "*OKAY! THANK YOU!*" and grab the wheel away from you, just in the nick of time, it seemed to me. After a moment during which he quietly regained his composure, he would say, "Good job. You did just fine."

My father let Sharla help first, saying I could have a turn on the way home. "Age has its privileges," he told me.

I said nothing, sat sulking by the window. I *knew* age had its privileges; I was witness to that fact practically every day of my life, courtesy of Sharla. But soon I lost myself looking in other people's windows. I liked pretending I lived in every house we passed. But I liked even better coming back to the knowledge that I lived where I did. I was happy; I knew this.

At Dairy Queen, we found one of the tiny picnic tables empty and claimed it. We sat eating our cones and watching the lines of people stepping up to the window and walking away with their prizes. I liked best seeing what the fat people got.

One very tall man came away from the window with a chili dog, which I had always wanted to try; but we never went to Dairy Queen for dinner. Occasionally it occurred to me to request a chili dog instead of ice cream, but that would have felt uncomfortable, improper. Dairy Queen was for ice cream and dessert, that was all. It was a rule in our family, and therefore law in the world.

It was a little unsettling not to have my mother there with us; the table was unbalanced. There was not a child and a parent on each side, as we were used to. Our father sat on my side, and though I was grateful for this, I felt bad for Sharla, who seemed deserted. It was also too quiet. My mother was the one who always initiated conversation, and then did what she needed to keep it going. A silent table was the sign of a lazy hostess, she always said. I felt obliged to substitute for her. I turned to my father, cleared my throat, and asked, "Do you like your job?"

"Do I like my *job*?" my father said. He shrugged. "I don't know."

I laughed.

"I'm serious," he said.

"What do you mean, you don't know?" Sharla asked.

He looked at her. "I mean . . . Well, I guess I don't really see the sense in thinking about things like whether I like my job. I like the people I work with. I like the view from my office window. But I don't think about whether I like the job itself."

"I'll bet everybody else knows if they like their job!" I said, although I had no idea.

"I don't think so," he said. "You just do it, that's all. You have to do it. You do it so you can buy Dairy Queen."

I smiled.

"Right?"

"Yup," I said. And then, "But what do you *do* at your job?"

"Talks on the phone and goes to meetings," Sharla said quickly. She had once gone to work for a morning with my father. I had been so ill with a summer cold my mother feared pneumonia; and at the last minute one weekday morning, she decided to take me to the doctor. My father took Sharla with him to work. She never let me forget it.

"Talks on the phone about what?" I persisted. "What does he talk about?"

"Insurance," my father said.

I was starting to get angry. "Yes, but what *about* insurance? Like, someone calls and they say . . . well, what *do* they say?"

"How about a horse bite?" my father said, moving his hand toward me.

I sighed, pulled my leg away from him.

"Well, then, how about walking on your head?"

"No!" I could just see myself in front of all the Dairy Queen customers as my father turned me upside down and held me by my ankles. He hadn't done this in years, but you never knew. "No," I said again.

"Well, it'll have to be a horse bite, then." He reached out and squeezed just above my knee. I howled in agonized pleasure.

On the way home, my father told Sharla and me he was giving us a raise in our allowance. He was going to up us to a dollar a week.

"I think I should get more," Sharla said.

"Why is that?"

"I'm older."

"Do you do more work?"

She stayed quiet.

"No, she does not," I said.

"Yes, I *do!*"

"Nuh-uh, you do *less*."

"Keep it up and I'll give you both a pay cut instead of a raise," my father said. Sharla and I stopped talking, but I felt her fingers pinching my thigh. I did nothing back. I was driving. I was thirty-five years old and behind the wheel of a car like Jasmine's. I owned a cheetah and sold perfume at a fancy store. My husband was a millionaire and a veterinarian, which was convenient, considering the cheetah.

When we got home, my father went into the living room, bent down, and kissed my mother's forehead. She was lying on the sofa, eyes closed. But when she felt his touch she reached up and put her hand on his shoulder.

He stood, turned toward us. "Want to go get something for me?" he asked. "Both of you?"

We nodded, dumb with shame and hope. He was going to kiss her. On the lips. That's how they did it, they always found a way for us not to see. Of course we did see anyway, sometimes. It paid to practice the stealth of Indians.

"Go in my top dresser drawer and you'll find a little brown envelope. Bring it down here, please."

We headed upstairs, taking our time, as we knew we were supposed to do.

I went to the right side of the dresser, Sharla to the left. I found nothing but handkerchiefs in the top drawer, and so I pulled open the drawer below it. There were many socks, all folded neatly and organized by color, but again no envelope. I rooted around a little, felt something, pulled it out, and gasped. Rubbers. The same yellow kind Jasmine had. I stuffed them back in among the socks, then stood staring down.

"Shut that!" Sharla said. She had opened the T-shirt drawer on the opposite side of the dresser, and now she pulled out the little brown envelope that lay on top. "*This* is what he meant!" she said. "It's right here where he said it was! What are you digging around for?"

"Did you see what I saw?" I asked.

She looked away, closed the T-shirt drawer. "You were looking in the wrong place."

"Yes, but did you—"

"Shut up!" She leaned over, slammed the sock drawer shut.

I could have reported her. We weren't allowed to say that. I think she knew I wouldn't say anything, though.

When we came back downstairs, my father was in his chair with the newspaper, my mother sitting up with a magazine. But it was clear they'd been kissing, all right; his lips were stained pink, and both of them had messy hair. My father pulled two silver dollars out of the brown envelope and gave one to Sharla and one to me. Then, smiling, he gave one to my mother. "*Thank* you!" she said. She looked as pleased as we were. I knew she would put the money in her "bank"—she kept a mayonnaise jar in the laundry room and filled it with change she found in the sofa. Periodically, she would convert it into paper money and then store that in an old purse she kept in her closet. She said she was saving for new carpeting.

Later that night, we played Monopoly and I won, because everybody underestimates the value of Baltic and

Mediterranean. It was no fun beating my parents, because they wanted me to win. But wiping out Sharla's funds, that was satisfying. Sometimes when she lost she would cry. Not tonight though. Tonight she forced a yawn and said she was tired of playing, anyway; thank God the game was over.

"Don't take the Lord's name in vain," my mother said.

"I'm not."

My mother sighed.

"I'm *not*! If I had said, 'God, I'm happy the game is over,' *that* would have been taking His name in vain. But I was just thanking Him."

My mother stared at her. Then, "I suppose you're right," she said. "Fine. So long as you know the difference."

After we went to bed, Sharla and I didn't talk about what I'd found in my father's drawer. Neither of us spoke at all. I thought perhaps each of us was waiting for the other to bring it up. Instead, we both fell asleep. In the early morning light, I lay awake, wondering if I'd only dreamed it. When finally I heard the rustling sounds of Sharla waking up, I asked, "Did you see what I found in Dad's drawer last night?"

"So what? Everybody has them who does sex."

"You knew they were there? You've seen them before?"

"No. But everybody has them."

I wasn't so sure. But I let it go in the way that you decide you don't really want something you can't reach.

I look at my watch. Halfway to San Francisco. I wonder how Sharla will look. Last time we met, I hadn't seen her in six months, and I was surprised by a new short-short hairdo she had. I couldn't believe she hadn't told me about it. "Didn't I," she said. "I was sure I had. Wait—I did! You said you were thinking of doing it yourself!"

"I did not!" I said. "I would never do that!" And then, quickly, "Not that it doesn't look good on you." It did look good on her, from certain angles. But on the whole, I thought it made her look older. Of course, we *are* older. This is something that is always sneaking up and shocking me. Sharla said recently that she could tell how much older she was getting not by how many wrinkles she had, but how many regrets.

"*That's* a pretty grim way of thinking," I said, when she told me.

"It's true, though, don't you think?"

"I don't know. I guess I don't really have that many regrets. I really like my life. I like the choices I've made."

"Oh come on," she said. "Don't you regret not going to Woodstock now more than ever?"

"Well, *yeah,* that's true. Yeah. I should have gone to Tahiti for the winter with Dennis Erickson that one time,

107

too. I really should have. He bought me a ticket and everything."

"We should have done a lot more dangerous things."

"I suppose."

"And we also should have . . . I don't know. I guess as I get older I feel more . . . generous in my heart. You know?"

I said nothing.

"Ginny?" she said gently, and I knew exactly where she was headed.

"I think some things are too hard to forgive," I said. "And I think some things don't deserve to be forgiven." I felt as though I were saying something I'd said so many times that the words had lost their meaning entirely. And yet I also felt I meant them.

I wonder now—chilly thought—if some of Sharla's longing to forgive, to come to terms, has to do with the fact that she knew even then that she was going to get seriously ill.

I look at my watch again.

My mother said she found the measure of time interesting. Another lie. I'm sure she found it terrifying.

The next Correspondence Day, there was no watching *Walt Disney World* until our letters were complete. I sat at the dining-room table jiggling my heel, chewing at the side of my thumb, staring wide-eyed into space. I had absolutely nothing to tell my grandparents, even though this was my week to write to my father's parents, who were easier to write to because they were less critical than my mother's parents. I'd selected the pale-blue stationery and black fountain pen, opened with the standard, "Hi! How are you???" but nothing further had come to me. It had been my practice to describe meals we'd eaten during the past week, but I was growing tired of that, mainly because the menus lately did not vary enough to make for good copy. I'd told my grandparents about Jasmine moving in, and there was nothing new to say about that, either—at least to them. I'd said I was looking forward to school in the last letter I'd sent them, though this was very much untrue.

There were certain things about school that I enjoyed: buying supplies, sniffing newly mimeographed papers, writing on the blackboard, staring into the teachers' lounge when I passed by it. I liked blowing straw wrappers across cafeteria tables. I also enjoyed sharpening pencils and watching movies in classrooms with the shades pulled down. Other than that, I hated it. I thought school was an unhealthy thing for a growing child, what with the way it demanded shoes on hot days, and wearing dresses, and sitting still at a wooden desk for hours at a time. With the exception of science, I did not find any of my subjects particularly relevant, and I stared out the windows in every classroom with a sense of desperation that often made me feel like crying. I could only bear to look at the teachers if there was something interesting about their outfit or hairdo or face, and there rarely was. On the day my English teacher, Mr. Purdy, cut himself shaving and wore an intriguing arrangement of tiny Band-Aids, I watched him for the length of the entire class. I knew some kids loved their teachers, and I couldn't begin to understand why; to me, they were only tall cellmates.

Still, I did well enough in school, earning mostly Bs and the occasional A. This was largely because I did homework with an intense kind of concentration that I did not display inside the walls of Foster Elementary. I liked doing homework because Sharla liked doing it— we would lie on our beds after school with books and papers scattered all around us. I would watch the precise way Sharla turned the pages of her textbook, and I would imitate her, down to turning exactly when she did. You licked your finger delicately before turning a page, then lifted it from the bottom right-hand corner. It was important to turn the page slowly and then smooth the center of the book with the flat of your hand. I read my pages so that I would have something to do until it was time to turn them again. Sharla read much more slowly than I; therefore I often read a page twice, or even three times. She never noticed my turning pages exactly when she did; I thought this was a very pleasant miracle.

My mother, who was not daydreaming like I was, licked an envelope, stamped it, and put it on the bottom of her little pile. Then she capped her pen and pushed her chair back from the table.

"Are you done already?" I asked.

"We've been here for over forty minutes."

"Who'd you write to?" Sharla asked. My mother corresponded with a number of relatives as well as friends she'd had since high school. It was always interesting to hear her talk about what she'd written; often, of course, her news featured us.

"Oh, Sandy Wertheimer," she said. "And Mom and Dad, of course. I told them about your recitals coming up. And the forts you've been building—my goodness, they're wonderful. Did either of you mention them?"

"Who else?" I asked.

"Pardon?"

"Who else did you write to? You have three envelopes."

She pulled her pile toward her, smiled. "Such a busybody. Who are *you* writing to?"

I sighed. "Grandma and Grandpa. They're the only ones I ever write to. There *isn't* anybody else to write to."

"Well, finish up," she said. "Then I'll walk these to the corner and mail them." This was something my mother had started doing recently. She used to clothespin letters outside for our mailman to take the next day, but lately she'd started going to the mailbox, three blocks away, at night. My father had initially offered to go with her, but she refused, saying she liked the "thinking time." "What do you think about?" he'd asked, and she'd said, "Oh, this and that; you know."

"Recipes, I'll bet," my father had said the first night she went out without him. He was standing at the window with his hands in his pockets, watching her walk away.

"What about recipes?" I'd asked. Sharla and I were right beside him. "Nothing," he'd said. "I was just . . . nothing."

My mother stood. "I'm going to go get my sweater. I'll be down in a little while to get your letters."

The promise of imminent release spurred me into action. I quickly wrote a paragraph about the last four dinners I could remember, describing in some detail the delicate suspension of fruit cocktail in the cherry Jell-O that had served as a salad last night. I liked Jasmine's idea of a salad much better: one afternoon I'd found her sitting down to a Caesar salad for lunch. I'd never heard of that, and I told her so.

"Really?" she'd said. And then she'd shown me how she had rubbed the cut edge of a clove of garlic over the inside of the big wooden bowl that was on her table. She described for me all the ingredients that went into the dressing as though she were reciting a love poem to someone in the dark. She picked up a large narrow leaf of lettuce, pale green, which she ate with her fingers; then she sucked them off. She shared the salad with me, encouraged me to eat it the same way. I did, though it embarrassed me. But it was delicious, the residue of that dressing licked from my own salty flesh.

My mother came back to the table, sat down to wait. I ended my letter with a wish that my grandparents would come and visit for a long time—mainly so that then I would not have to write to them. I licked the envelope, stamped it, and handed it to my mother. I could hardly wait to live in my own house, where I would never write one letter to anyone, ever.

"Sharla?" my mother said. "Are you finished?"

Sharla folded her letter—two pages, front and back!— put it in an envelope, and handed it to my mother. I hated the teacher's-pet look on her face, I hated it when she got this way. She folded her hands and rested them on top of the table. Below it, I assumed her feet were lined up exactly even with each other.

"What did you write about?" I asked. Four pages!

"What I want for Christmas."

"It's August!"

"So?"

"Isn't that cheating?" I asked my mother.

"It's fine." She smiled at Sharla. "I assume, however, that you talked about other things, as well. Such as Grandma and Grandpa, I assume you asked about them."

Sharla nodded gravely.

My mother nodded, too. Then, "I'll be right back," she said.

"You cheated," I told Sharla, as soon as I heard the door close behind my mother.

"I did not."

"Huh. Anybody can write about what they want for Christmas."

"You're just mad because you didn't think of it."

This was true. Therefore I changed the subject. "Who else did Mom write to?" It had occurred to me that the

letter she would not show me had something to do with
my birthday. It wasn't far away, and I was beginning
to think everything that happened, more or less, had something to do with it. I had yet to make a formal list of
things that I wanted, but my mother might be sending
away for some wonderful surprise. Last time she had
done that, I'd gotten a monogrammed towel set, which I
loved so much I wouldn't use it.

"She wrote to Jasmine," Sharla said, and yawned,
stretching her arms up high over her head. "I saw when
she addressed the envelope."

"Why? She lives next *door*!"

Sharla shrugged. "She's not here now. Maybe Mom
had something to tell her."

"She'll be *back* in a couple *days*!"

"I know." She stood. "I'm going to make a cake for
Dad. Want to help?"

I stood, too, pushed my chair in. "Yeah. For Mom and
Dad, you mean."

"No. Just for Dad."

I stopped, stared at her. "Why not Mom, too?"

"Do you want to help or not?"

"Yeah. Dibs on the frosting part."

"Half. You can frost the bottom half."

"Can I break the egg?" I asked, when we were in the
kitchen.

Sharla opened the refrigerator, handed me an egg. We
worked in silence. I wanted to ask Sharla something, but
I didn't know what. When our mother came back, she
asked what we were doing, and Sharla told her. "Ah,"
she said. "How nice! It's for . . . nothing, then?"

"It's because he's Dad," Sharla said—coldly, I thought.

My mother stood still for a moment, smiling. Then, "Well," she said, "that's very nice of you."

She went into the living room, and I heard her and my father talking under the blare of the television. The words got louder, then stopped abruptly; then I heard the faint click of my mother's knitting needles. It came to me to put pop beads on my birthday list; I really wanted some of those. It was a relief, thinking of something so easy.

I awakened several mornings later to the sound of Jasmine's and my mother's voices coming from the kitchen, then noticed a third voice as well—a boy's. I thought it must be someone asking about mowing the lawn, or selling some utterly unwantable thing for the Boy Scouts, but the conversation was going on too long for that. I turned to ask Sharla if she knew who was downstairs, but found her bed empty. Then I heard the toilet flush, and she came back to bed, yawned. "What?" she said.

"Who's down there?"

She shrugged.

"Did you hear a boy's voice?"

"Well, *yeah*, they're *talking* loud enough! I wanted to sleep some more, too. I was up really late last night."

"No, you weren't." We had gone to bed at the boring hour of ten o'clock.

"Yes I was! I got up after you were already asleep. I was reading."

I checked her face; she was telling the truth. "Reading what?"

She pulled a book from under her covers. It was *Beautiful Joe*, a book about a dog that Uncle Roy had brought with him last Thanksgiving, and which neither Sharla nor I had ever really looked at. Now, since Sharla was interested, so was I.

"Is it good?" I asked.

She nodded. "I cried."

"You did?"

She nodded again.

"Can I read it when you're done?"

"I am done."

I held out my hand.

She pulled the book to her chest. "I might want to read it again."

"Well, just let me read it first."

"No, I might want to read it again right *away*."

I knew what I needed to do: feign disinterest. But I could not. "Just give it to me first. I read way faster than you. I'll give it back in a day or two."

"No."

"Then I'm just taking it." I got up, started toward her bed.

"MOOOOMMMMMM!" Sharla yelled.

I sat back down, slack-jawed. We had company!

I heard the creak of the stairs; and then my mother, wearing a new red print housedress and her favorite yellow apron, came into our room. She said nothing. She didn't need to. The expression on her face talked. She was wearing makeup, a rarity at this time of day; I saw the faint traces of rouge on her cheeks, and her lashes were longer, as they were when she used her mascara. That mascara came in a small, red lacquered box. There was a rectangular cake of mascara and a cunning little brush you used to apply it. I couldn't imagine why my mother didn't use it constantly. When I was old enough to use makeup, I intended to sleep in it.

My mother put her hands on her hips. "Well?"

"She started it," I said.

"We have a guest," my mother answered. Her voice sounded different to me. Happier, I realized; that was the difference. Sharla and I were fighting, but she was still happy.

"Who's here?" I asked.

"It's Jasmine's nephew, a very nice boy named Wayne."

Wayne! I had never met a boy named *Wayne*! The name seemed exotic to me, and slightly disgusting. Sissified. I liked plain names for boys: Bill. Tom. Pete. Whenever Sharla and I staged scenes featuring a male character, we used names like that. Wayne and I would not be able to be friends.

"I want you two to get dressed," my mother said. "Then come down and say hello. I'll get breakfast started."

One thing I hated about company was the way your routine always had to get altered—I liked change only when I initiated it. I didn't like getting dressed to eat breakfast; it made the food taste different. I liked not even washing my face or brushing my teeth first, if the truth be told. I liked to be as close to the sleep state as possible, then let the colors and smells and sights of breakfast foods be my wake-up, rather than the rude splash of water. I did this on school days, too—came down and ate breakfast first, then got dressed. Sharla was the opposite: when she came to the table on school mornings, she was ready to go, down to her hair ribbon being perfectly tied and her well-organized book bag lying at her feet like an obedient dog. She might eat breakfast without getting dressed in the summer, but only after she had washed her face, brushed her teeth, and combed her hair.

"How can you drink *orange* juice when you just brushed your *teeth*?" I would often ask her, as though perhaps at some point my question would initiate change in her. "How can you be such a slob?" she would answer, hoping no doubt that her response might elicit the same in me. Neither of us changed, of course; and when we were at the breakfast table together, we sat eyeing each other with mutual disgust and superiority.

My mother started to leave, then turned back. "I'll expect you downstairs in ten minutes."

"Bathroom first," Sharla said. I dressed while she was in there; then, when it was my turn, I went to wash resentfully. When I dried my face off, I noticed a piece of sleep clinging stubbornly to the corner of my right eye. I left it there, then brushed my teeth without toothpaste. So there. I sighed, sat for a moment on the closed lid of the toilet. It was only morning, and I was already in a bad mood.

When we came into the kitchen, I saw a tall boy standing at the kitchen window, his back to us. "Well. *Here* are my girls," my mother said. The boy turned around and I saw that he was the person in the picture Jasmine kept in her dresser drawer. I put my hand to my eye quickly, removed the sleep.

My mother made her introductions. Wayne Meyers was his whole name. I said, "Hi," waved loosely, and looked away. Sharla moved to sit in the chair closest to him. "How long are you here for?" she asked, in a tone of voice that I did not recognize. She was smiling prettily.

"Two weeks." He smiled back at her. I put him at about fourteen, but he spoke with the ease of an adult.

"Well, come and sit *down*, Ginny," Jasmine said, laughing, indicating the seat beside her. I sat, then stared at my knees. Wayne was an extremely handsome boy; he had no business at my breakfast table. I had no idea what to do next. I felt as though something had hold of my shoulders and was pushing down. Something else worked at my center, pulling at my insides like taffy.

"Jasmine and I are going into town for a while," my mother said. "We were hoping you could show Wayne around the neighborhood a bit."

I looked up. "Well. . . . There's not much to show." For the first time, I hated where I lived.

"We could walk to the record store," Sharla said brightly.

"We could go out into the woods," I said.

There was a moment of weighted silence, and then Wayne said, "Why don't we do both?"

I saw my mother and Jasmine smile at each other. "Ready for some scrambled eggs?" my mother asked.

"I don't care," I said. "I'm not hungry." This was a lie, but I knew girls were supposed to have tiny appetites. Tiny appetites, small waists, friendly personalities, and no BO. Sharla said she wanted a lot to eat, however. She said she was starving. I looked out of the corner of my eye at Wayne. He was not shocked, or disgusted, or disappointed. He was sitting down, reaching for a piece of the toast that was already on the table.

"Can we have bacon, too?" I asked. My mother tightened her apron around her waist. She was smiling a little,
though I was sure she was unaware of this. She always
smiled when she was feeding people; she loved doing it.
Every time she baked, she'd tie small bundles of extras
onto the mailbox for the carrier. She made the cakes that
fetched the greatest sums at our school's bake sales; they
were famous for their height, their rich flavors, and their
whimsical decorations: fresh flowers, old jewelry, a
paper doll wearing a tiny cloth apron, feet rooted in the
frosting. She got a little nervous about going to dinner
parties unless they were potlucks; at those times, she was
always ready to go before my father was. It seemed her
contribution was what made her valid.

Now she laid strips of bacon in the frying pan, cracked
eggs into a yellow bowl. She beat them vigorously, then
came to the table with the coffeepot to refill Jasmine's cup.

"Thanks, Marion," Jasmine said, and there was something in the rich tone of her voice that had me look
quickly at her, then away. An image came to me: a hand
pushing into folds of black velvet, a hidden discovery.

I pulled my chair closer to the table, straightened my
fork and knife, put my glass of orange juice directly over
the knife, where it belonged. Then I put my hands in my
lap to wait. Polite. Proper. "Where's Dad?" I asked.

"At work, silly," my mother said. "You know that."

So I did. He was at work, missing the party. Not even
knowing if he liked where he was or not.

At five o'clock that evening, Sharla and I were seated at
the kitchen table, shucking corn for dinner. I hated this
job because I had once found a worm when I was doing

it, and I was sure it would happen again. But my mother was frying chicken and the aroma made up for my discomfort. She used many spices for frying chicken, among them tarragon, ginger, and rosemary. But she always added things quickly, and so it was hard to see everything that she used. Once I asked her, but she wouldn't tell me. She said, "Oh, it's a secret. I couldn't tell you all the ingredients. It wouldn't turn out anymore if I did." She seemed to be both joking and not; I did not pursue it. Sharla said our mother wouldn't tell what went into many of her recipes because *she* didn't know; she just made things up. I didn't see why she couldn't admit that, if it were true.

After I cleaned the last ear of corn, I laid some of the whitish silk across the top of my head. "I am a sun-streaked blonde," I said. "I am on the cover of *Life*." No response, not from Sharla or my mother. I moved the silk to rest under my nose. "I am a man," I said narrowly, through my pooched lips. They both looked at me, then away.

I pulled the corn silk off my face. "I am a man in a circus," I said loudly. "I train animals that would just as soon kill you both as look at you."

"Uh-huh," my mother said, turning the chicken pieces carefully.

"They would kill you if they would kill us," Sharla said.

"No," I said, "they would not. Because I would know how to charm them, and they would love me."

"Huh, they would eat you first, because you're so annoying," Sharla said.

She was mad at me. As far as I could figure, it was because Wayne had liked me better than her. Sharla had tried to show off at the record store, pretending to know more than she did. But Wayne noticed that she confused Fabian with Pat Boone, and she shut up after that, sulked all the way home.

When we had all gone into the woods, Sharla had hung around listlessly for a while, then gone inside the house. At first, I felt guilty, imagining her lying on her bed, bored, holding her arm up in the air to watch the charms on her bracelet dangle. But then I forgot about her. The truth was, meeting Wayne had let me see that I was tired of Sharla's company. I recognized in Wayne a kindred spirit. His gaze lingered on the things I found interesting, too: a bent-over woman wearing a print kerchief on her head and crossing the street with achy slowness; a shop window with merchandise arranged into the shape of a pyramid; a truck with a canvas flap blowing open as it took a corner. Wayne liked to read. He picked up a shiny penny he passed on the sidewalk, pronouncing it lucky, then gave it to me.

In some ways, I could hardly stand being with him; it was too new and too much. But I also wanted to be nowhere else. I felt thirsty and thirsty; I felt hungry and hungry. I wanted to show him everything in my box hidden in the closet; I wanted to have a picnic with him; I hoped he'd try to kiss me on the mouth. I was ready, suddenly, to be kissed. My stomach ached mildly, then occasionally leaped up as though it were being poked. I guessed I had a boyfriend. I guessed, actually, that I was in love. I couldn't stop smiling, though I had enough self-control not to show my teeth.

I knew Sharla was very much taken with Wayne, too, but it didn't matter: clearly, she was not his type. She

only went for his looks. When he showed her a mocking-
bird, she barely looked, missing entirely the fabulous
white bars on the wings. When he told a joke, her laughter sounded false. When he told her he was a magician,
she did not inquire as to his repertoire; and when I did
so, she listened only to be polite—I could tell by the fixed
expression on her face. But for me, things were opening
like a flower.

We had eaten lunch at Woolworth's. Wayne and I got
patty melts and coffee—the latter after Wayne told the
sleepy-eyed waitress that we both had hypothyroidism
and needed to drink it to stay alive. Sharla, tight-lipped,
ordered a tuna salad sandwich and milk. After the waitress left, Wayne and I had talked about her earrings, how
they didn't match—one was a gold knot, the other a blue
rhinestone flower. We wondered if it could possibly have
been intentional; then, why that might have been so.
"Maybe she wants to get fired," I said. "Maybe her boss
is mean."

"Maybe she has two personalities," Wayne said. "Two
names. Two houses."

Sharla hadn't noticed the earrings. At that point, it
was clear to me—and to her, too, apparently, since she
stopped trying to make any kind of conversation—that
Wayne was all mine.

So after we got home and Sharla went in the house, I
had brought Wayne to our tepee, and he lay down in the
center of it. I sat off to the side, cross-legged, in peaceful
silence. Outside, buffalo roamed.

Wayne closed his eyes, breathed in deeply, then raised
himself up on one elbow to look at me. "You want to get
married?" he asked.

"I—what?"

"Do you want to get married?"

What did this mean, I wondered. "Are you kidding?"

"No." There was, in his blue eyes, a steadiness older than both of us. I felt as though my real name had at last been spoken, my self cracked open unto myself. There was something inside me—not quite developed, but there nonetheless: a potential, a bud of my coming self that he recognized, and it responded to him. I believed he had a kind of rightness and wisdom. Instinctively, I trusted him—without reason, without thought, without care.

But *married*! "You mean, when we grow up?" I asked.

"No."

"We can't get married now; we're too young." I couldn't believe I was saying words like these. It felt as if birds could fly down and pluck jewels from my mouth.

"No, we aren't," Wayne said. "We're just too young to use a minister. So we'll do the ceremony ourselves."

I said nothing. My heart was stretched. I felt as though I were either going to start crying or laugh out loud.

"It wouldn't be a real marriage," he said.

"I know."

"It wouldn't be legal, I mean."

"Oh. Yes."

"But . . . otherwise, it would be real." He lay down again, closed his eyes. "You're the one for me."

"I am?"

"Yes."

"How do you know?"

He turned his head, looked at me. "Don't you?"

"I'm only twelve," I said. "Well, soon I will be."

"Yes. I'm fifteen."

We stared at each other. I heard the faint drone of an airplane. A dog barked, then barked again; a car door slammed.

Finally, I looked away, drew a faint line in the dirt, laid my hand on top of it.

"We'll have a ceremony tonight," he said. "Meet me here at midnight."

Midnight! Well, there you had it. It was meant to be. I took my hand off the tentative line I'd made in the dirt, etched the line deeper, drew a circle around it. "Look," I said, wanting something.

Wayne studied my drawing, nodded once; twice. Then he drew another line in the circle, parallel to mine, the same size exactly, and looked up at me. I nodded back slowly. A foreign word wanted out of my mouth. "Ahuna," I said. "Ahuna," he said back, then whispered, "Take nana." And then neither of us moved for a long time.

I was alive with love, generous because of it, and so I tried to make up to Sharla for taking the only available boy of the summer. "Want me to help you finish cleaning the corn?" I asked.

She shrugged.

I took a fat ear from her, shucked it carefully. It was so easy to be wonderful to others when someone thought you were special. *Ginny Meyers,* I thought. I didn't like the sound of it, really. But that was small, that was a very small thing, compared to the expanding personal universe inside my chest.

My mother was leaning against the kitchen counter, arms crossed, looking out the window and daydreaming.

"Hey, Mom," I said. I didn't like it when she daydreamed; it made her not continuously available to me. "Mom!"

She startled, looked over at me. "What?"

"What are you doing?"

"Nothing." She began washing the dishes that were piled in the sink.

"It's your birthday soon," I said. "And then mine."

She smiled. "Yes, it is. Are you sure you want the same thing for dinner again?"

In our family, you got to have anything you wanted to eat on your birthday. You got to not make your bed, to forgo all of your chores and lessons, in fact—I was living for the day my birthday fell on a dance class day. You also got to skip school if you wanted. Since my birthday fell in the summer, I got to skip any day of the school year. I always wanted to pick the first day, but never could. Therefore I usually picked the last. And, since age four, I had always picked the same thing for my dinner.

"I want what I always have," I said. I loved my mother's enchiladas. I always got to eat one of mine when she had just wrapped them, before they were baked. "Can I eat all of mine raw this time?" I asked.

"It's your birthday."

"Then I won't have any dinner when you eat yours."

"You'll have some rice and beans."

"Okay. And I want caramel frosting on my cake. Caramel."

"I know. And a white cake, in the shape of a star. And pink candles."

Well, I had to be sure. She'd been so dreamy lately. I thought maybe she'd better start getting more sleep.

She poked at the chicken, then took off her apron. "I'll be right back."

"Where are you going?" Sharla asked.

"Just to borrow something from Jasmine." She turned down the flame under the chicken, covered it. "This should be fine, but keep an eye on it."

We watched from the window as she knocked on Jasmine's door, then entered without waiting for Jasmine to open it. "They're best friends now," Sharla said, sighing.

"I know."

"I wish I had a best friend like her."

"Me, too." I thought of Wayne; maybe I *had* found a friend like her. Only more.

Sharla turned to me, spoke in a low voice. "Jasmine gave me a gold bracelet, don't tell Mom."

"She did?"

Sharla nodded. "It has a *diamond* on it."

"Huh. I doubt it."

"It *does*. It's real, too, she told me."

"Can I see it?"

"After we go to bed."

"Well . . . okay." I was worried. I had something to do after we went to bed: get married. I'd make sure Sharla showed me the bracelet right after we turned in; then she'd be asleep by midnight.

After about ten minutes, my mother returned from Jasmine's empty-handed. "What did you get?" I asked.

"Pardon?" She lifted the lid on the chicken, covered it again.

"What did you get? From Jasmine. You said you were going to borrow something."

She stared at me blankly. Then she said, "Before a birthday, some things are secret."

"All we *talk* about is her *birth*day," Sharla said. "*Everybody* has a *birth*day."

"Shut up," I said quietly.

"What did you say?" my mother asked.

"She said, 'Shut up,' " Sharla answered.

"I have told you I do not want to hear that kind of talk in this house."

I shrugged.

"Apologize to your sister, Ginny."

"Sorry," I said. And, actually, I was. I felt bad for Sharla. She didn't have a boyfriend and her birthday wasn't until December.

"Jasmine asked if you girls wanted to go to the movie with her and Wayne tonight."

"I do," I said quickly.

"What a shock," Sharla said. And then, "I'll go, too. If you don't mind." She smiled at me then, a small, sad smile, and I knew she was giving him to me completely.

"Yes, of course I want you to come," I told her. I sat back in my chair, pleased with myself.

"Want to make me a French twist before we go?" Sharla asked.

"Okay." I would be so gentle.

"Should we do our nails after that?"

"Sure!"

"Use that red if you want to," my mother called after us as we headed up the stairs. "It's in the medicine chest."

This stopped both Sharla and me in our tracks. Not long ago, we had brought home a bright red polish from

Woolworth's. "Well. It's very pretty, but I don't think *quite* yet," my mother had said, and she had taken the polish away to "save" for us. (She was also "saving" a strapless bra a friend of Sharla's had given her, as well as a paperback book called *Real Treasure*, which I'd brought home from the drugstore. The cover featured a bare-chested pirate standing next to a busty woman in lovely distress.)

"When can we have red?" I'd asked.

"When you are eighteen," she'd answered, her standard response.

Suddenly, things were different.

Sharla and I moved quickly up the stairs, before she changed her mind.

The flight attendant asks if I would like something to drink. Sure, about six more scotches. Instead, I ask for coffee, then stare out the window as I drink it. Far below me, I can see some birds flying in a raggedy formation. One of them looks different from the others, though from this distance I can't really tell for sure.

I used to fantasize that I'd be outside some day and see our parakeet, Lucky, flying illegally in some V-shaped squadron. I figured I'd hold up my finger, call his name, and he'd joyfully alight. Then I'd bring him home and give him a fancy bird treat.

It was soon after I'd met Wayne that Lucky had escaped. My mother had brought the cage into the backyard—to clean it, she said—and somehow he got out. We'd had the bird for five years, and we felt terrible, Sharla and I, and even Wayne—he'd helped us look for Lucky for hours. My mother said she felt bad, too, but I remember thinking there was something false in her saying so. At the time, I thought it was just that she didn't really care about pets. Now, sitting here and looking out the window into this vast sky, I realize something. She must have let him go. It would have fit, for her to have done something like that about that time. Of course she let him go.

As it happened, Jasmine did not go to the movie with us. Just before our turn at the ticket window, she said suddenly, "You know what? I think I'll just drop you guys off. You don't need me."

"Don't you want to see this?" I asked. It was *Ben Hur*. I couldn't imagine her walking away from this movie, just like that. Charlton Heston was in it!

"I'll see it some other time," she said. "Maybe your mother and I will go."

"She goes to the movies with my father," Sharla said, and my indignant heart leaped up in confirmation. They probably would have come tonight, in fact, if my father hadn't been working; they loved the movies.

"Well, maybe the three of us will go tomorrow night," Jasmine said. I supposed this was possible. My father seemed to genuinely like Jasmine. Only last week, he had spent an hour at her place fixing a drip in her kitchen sink; she had rewarded him with a new toolbox—both clasps were broken on his old one. And occasionally after dinner the three of them would sit in lawn chairs out in our yard and drink coffee together, swatting at the mosquitoes.

Jasmine bought our tickets, handed us each one. I hoped that the numbers on my stub would add up to

131

twenty-one, which meant I could kiss my boyfriend. Or eighteen, which gave you the right to a hug. Under the right circumstances, a hug would surely lead to a kiss. I had gotten twenty-one twice before; the tickets were taped uselessly into my scrapbook. Now I added my numbers while we waited in line for popcorn. I had twenty. That meant somebody else had something. I looked to see if Sharla was adding her numbers up. No. Not Wayne, either.

"Want to go to the bathroom?" I asked Sharla.

"No."

"Sure?"

She looked at me. "No!"

"Okay," I said, and stood immobile beside her.

"*Go,*" she said. "We'll wait."

I looked over at Wayne, who was busy buying pop-corn. "I just wanted to *ask* you something," I told Sharla quietly.

"Oh! Okay." She tapped Wayne on the shoulder, told him, "We're just going to the powder room." And then, pointing to her mouth, "Lipstick."

I admired Sharla's quick thinking. It wouldn't do for him to imagine us excusing ourselves for any other rea-son. Comfortable as I felt with him, there were limits.

"Why don't you go ahead and get seats?" I asked, as he came away from the counter. He'd gotten the large-size popcorn, a red-and-white-striped bucket approxi-mately the size of the pail my mother used to scrub floors. I inhaled the yellow smell of butter and salt, con-tent. We would bump knuckles.

"Where do you like to sit?" he asked.

I had no idea. No one had ever asked me.

"Middle section, middle of the row," Sharla said. "Not behind a bighead or a hat." Apparently she did think about it. And it came to me that that was why *I* didn't; I had always just played the role of the subordinate: the older sister decided, the younger one complied. Usually, with gratitude.

In the bathroom, Sharla pulled me into the corner by the paper-towel dispenser. "Did you get the curse?" she asked, her face close to mine.

I shook my head.

She pulled away, disappointed. "Well, what, then? Hurry up, the cartoon is going to start."

"What are the numbers on your ticket?" I asked.

"Oh." She checked her stub, then looked up at me, smiling. "Want to trade?"

"Is it twenty-one?" I asked, my breath coming out through a suddenly narrower passage.

"Bingo."

I took her stub, gave her mine.

"But are you sure?" she said. "Are you ready?"

I nodded, and we started walking. Then I stopped, took her arm. "Have you ever kissed anyone?"

She shook her head.

"Oh. Sorry."

"I've *hugged*," she said.

"Who?"

"Never mind; come on, I'll bet it's already started."

"*Who?*"

She sighed. "Steve Golinsky, okay? At Jane O'Connell's birthday party last month, spin the bottle, but I wouldn't kiss."

Steve Golinsky! I tried to think of something remarkable about him. Nothing came to me. He was a quiet boy, average-looking. A member of the chess club, brown tie shoes. But still, *Steve Golinsky!* my mind insisted, fueled by the image of a kiss.

"Why wouldn't you kiss?" I asked, a little worried.

"I didn't say *you* couldn't. *I* didn't want to, that's all."

I bit my lip, nodded. Steve Golinsky. I understood Sharla not wanting to do anything with him. But *Wayne*!

"Well, I think I'll do it," I said. "I will. I'm going to do it."

"I know." She shrugged, brushed a piece of hair back from my eyes. "You look pretty."

We walked out together toward the darkened theater, resolute as soldiers, both of us. This is the beginning, I was thinking. Right here. Of a lot.

We walked home, as we'd assured Jasmine we could. From the sidewalk outside our house, we saw my mother and her in the living room, seated on the sofa. My father's car was still gone; he was working very late.

When we opened the door, my mother jumped up. "You're back!" She walked quickly toward us, smoothing her skirt with the flat of her hands.

Sharla rolled her eyes at me.

"Yeah, we're back," I said.

"Would you like a snack?"

I looked at Wayne. I thought I knew exactly what he was thinking: why wasn't she asleep? When would she be?

"We had a lot of popcorn," Wayne said. "But thanks." I loved his boy blue jeans. I loved his white shirt and his brown belt, the way he got tiny crinkles around his eyes when he smiled, the way, when he looked down, his lashes made shadows on his cheeks.

Jasmine stood, stretched. "I guess I'll go on home to bed."

"It *is* late," I said.

Oh, and his teeth were white and straight, his hands warm—I'd held one the entire length of the movie. He had a smell that might have been cologne, but was not, I was sure; it was just him, just an invisible part of him that I wished would be made tangible and pocket-sized, so that I could have it and carry it with me everywhere. I'd walked close beside him all the way home; listened to his smooth, low voice tell jokes, ask questions of Sharla and me, share stories about his life back home. He was the pitcher on his high school baseball team; he'd won a blue ribbon at the county art show for a charcoal drawing he'd done of a shoe.

"A *shoe*!" Sharla had said, incredulous. "You won a *prize* from drawing a *shoe*?" But I was not surprised. All you had to do was really look at a shoe to see how much was there: the valleys in the creases of the leather, the graceful lines of the hanging laces, the implied history of the absent wearer.

My mother stood smiling, her hands clasped tightly together. I noticed dark circles under her eyes, and I checked her face for anything else, but there was nothing. She was not ill. She did not even appear to be tired, really.

Jasmine rose, put on her shoes, which I saw now had been left in a corner of the room. "I'll see you tomorrow, Marion," she said. "We'll plan the menu." She smiled at me as she walked past. I noticed the faint aroma of a new perfume.

Wayne waved at us, followed her out. "I'll see *you* later," his back told me. I'd shown him my ticket on the way home. He hadn't understood what the numbers meant at first; they didn't do that in Mobile. But he knew now.

"What menu is Jasmine talking about?" I asked my mother. I had to get my mind off Wayne for a minute, or I'd faint.

"Oh, for my Tupperware party," she said. "It's that time of year."

"What night will it be?" I liked Tupperware parties. My mother made fancy snacks we never got otherwise: cucumber sandwiches. Asparagus rolled in wafer-thin slices of ham. Small flowered dishes full of fat cashews.

"August seventeenth," she said, and began straightening the pillows on the sofa.

"That's your birthday!" Sharla said.

"Yes."

"Well, don't you want ... I don't know, it's your *birth*day!" Sharla was clearly frustrated by my mother's lack of attention to herself; I appreciated it, since it kept my birthday as the important one.

"I know that, Sharla. I'm aware of when my birthday is."

"Well, aren't you and Dad going out for dinner or something?"

"I don't know. The day before, I suppose we could. Or the day after, what difference does it make, really?"

Sharla and I stood still, stared at her. "We'll *go*," she

said, laughing. "Just not on the day itself. It doesn't *mat*ter."

Does so was at the back of my throat. Stuck there.

"I'm going to bed. Did you girls lock the door behind you?"

We hadn't. We didn't do that. Our father did that every night; then his large frame filled our doorway as he checked on us. Often, I'd been awake to see him. He kept one hand in his pants pocket, and he leaned against the doorjamb, just watching. I could hear him breathe, sometimes. And sometimes I could hear him sigh. I always wanted to talk to him then, to offer him some sort of reassurance that he seemed to need, but I didn't want to get in trouble for being awake. I missed him now, as though he'd been away for a very long time.

Then, as if in answer to a silent request, I saw headlights sweep across the ceiling, heard a car door slam. "Dad's home!" I said.

"Is he?" My mother was halfway up the stairs. She did not start back down.

I looked at Sharla, then at the empty staircase, then at my father coming through the front door. He looked tired: his tie was off, his rumpled shirt open a few buttons. But he looked good. He did, he looked good. "Mom just went up," I said. "Just now."

He glanced toward the stairs. "Okay," he said. And then, "What are you two doing up so late?"

"We saw a movie," Sharla said. "*Ben Hur.*"

"Ah. Yes, I want to see that one, too." He put his briefcase in the closet, arched his back, rubbed a shoulder.

"Are you tired?" I asked.

"Me? No. No, I'm fine."

He said that when he was sick, too. He would be in his plaid robe, face flushed with fever, flat on his back, and that is exactly what he would say.

I felt in my pocket for my ticket stub, forced a yawn. "I'm going upstairs," I said. My father crossed over to me, kissed the top of my head. "Sleep well."

Not hardly. I had so much to do it felt like an alarm clock had just gone off. I went into the bathroom. I wanted to comb my hair and put some Vaseline on my lips. It could look like lipstick, if you did it right.

When I came into our bedroom, I found Sharla sitting on my bed, holding a black box in her hand.

"Is that it?" I asked. "The bracelet?"

"Shhhh!" She nodded.

"Well, let me see."

She opened the box, lifted up a round gold bracelet, slipped it on. It was a bangle type, thin.

"I don't see any diamond," I said.

"It's here." She pointed to a place on the bracelet. I came closer, looked. It was there all right, a small stone.

"How do you know it's real?" I asked. "It looks just like a rhinestone."

Sharla looked at me, disgusted.

"It does!"

"Would Jasmine have a rhinestone bracelet?"

"She might."

Sharla sighed, took the bracelet off, put it back in the box. "I knew it."

"What?"

"I knew you would just be jealous."

"I'm not jealous." In fact I wasn't, but only because of Wayne.

Sharla sat, head bowed over her ruined prize.

"Could I try it on?" I asked.

Her spirits seemed to lift. She opened the box, held the bracelet out toward me. I slid it onto my wrist. It did have a certain something. I raised my arm, moved my wrist back and forth. The diamond flashed, fractured its light into small rainbows. "Fancy," I said. "Wow." I handed it back. Sharla returned it to its box, but kept the lid open, continued to look at the bracelet.

"Why don't you wear it?" I asked.

"I can't. If Mom and Dad see it, they'll make me give it back."

"What will you do with it, then?"

"Put it in the closet. When I get my own apartment, I'll wear it."

"That's so long to wait," I said. "Why don't you wear it just when you sleep?"

She thought about it, then put the bracelet on, smiled.

"It feels good, huh?"

She nodded, went over to her own bed, crawled in and turned away from me. "Night," she said, yawning.

I went to the window, looked out into the backyard to see if Wayne was there yet. He was. He sat still as a statue right in the middle of the yard, cross-legged, waiting. I was grateful my parents' windows faced the street. I put a nightgown over my clothes, got into bed, turned off our bedside lamp, listened for the sound of my parents talking. When they stopped, I'd wait a good fifteen minutes, then sneak out. I turned my head toward their room, held still, heard nothing.

But then the toilet flushed, the bathroom door opened, and someone walked down the hall. I heard my parents' bedroom door close softly. Now they would talk awhile, they always did: the soft rise and fall of their voices had always sounded to me like a lullaby; I rocked slowly to it in my bed, sometimes. I listened intently, heard nothing; listened harder, heard nothing still. I watched the clock until ten minutes had passed, then pulled off my nightgown, snuck down the stairs, and went out into the night.

Wayne stood up when he saw me coming, held out a hand, and I took it. We walked toward the woods, saying nothing. When we reached the tepee, Wayne went in and I followed.

"Are you ready?" he asked.

I nodded, felt my breath catch on a jag in my throat.

"Do you want me to start, or do you want to?"

I shrugged.

He pulled me close to him, lowered his face toward mine. "Close your eyes," he said.

"Why?"

"It's better that way."

"I want to see."

"You'll see," he said. "Close your eyes." And then, softer, "Close them."

I did. And I felt his breath on my face, then his mouth pressing down on mine. The effect of such absolute intimacy made me feel jerked from soft black into bright white, from my own backyard into someplace I'd never imagined. I felt as though I were drowning, unable to rise up from under his lips or his invisible spirit, which felt bigger than mine, and stronger. He ground his hips into me. It hurt, and I pulled away. "That's enough!"

He stood still. His breath came quick, as though he'd been running.

"That's all I want to do," I said.

He nodded, sat down.

I sat beside him, stared straight ahead, breathed in once, twice. Then I pulled his face toward me again, closed my eyes, and found his mouth. This time, I relaxed; and I thought if I wanted to, I could die a good death this very moment, float up as my whole self in my red shorts and plaid shirt and bare feet, right into heaven. Wayne's arms tightened around my waist; we lay down smoothly. I could smell the earth and feel it beneath me, too: other arms, in a way; just as welcome.

We kissed again, then again; and then I heard the sound of someone walking, and froze. "Just keep still," Wayne whispered. "They won't see us. Keep quiet."

I did, but I kept my eyes open. And what I saw through the door of the tepee was my mother, standing in the backyard, dressed in her nightgown and slippers. She was talking softly, saying something I couldn't make out. I looked for someone near her, but saw no one; it appeared she was talking to herself. She quieted, then held still, lifted her chin as though she were being addressed by someone above her. Then, unbelievably, she began flapping her arms like wings, and walking about in circles. I was horribly embarrassed. I turned to Wayne, who was quietly watching. "She's never done this," I whispered. "She has *never* done *this*."

He nodded.

"I don't know *what* she's doing!"

He shrugged. "She's not doing anything. She's just goofing around."

I looked back at her. She was still now, facing Jasmine's house. And then she walked toward it, disappeared into the darkness.

I cleared my throat, laughed a little. And then I lay down, covered my face with my hands. I felt Wayne leaning over me; he was trying to pry my hands off my face. "Ginny," he said.

"No!" I kept my face covered. I wanted to talk to Sharla. I needed my father.

"Hey, Ginny," Wayne said. "Look! *Quick!*"

I pulled my hands off my face.

"It's me," he said, smiling.

I smiled back in spite of myself. "I *know.*"

"Come on. Let's go outside." We went around in back of the tepee, sat on the ground.

He picked a blade of grass, then pulled gently at it as though he were persuading it to stretch. "They just act crazy sometimes," he said. "Mothers. It's just that most people never see them acting that way—they do it alone. If you hadn't been out here with me, you wouldn't have seen it either."

"I'll bet your mother never acts like that," I said.

"My mother . . ."

"What?"

"Nothing. Never mind." He laid the piece of grass across the palm of his hand, blew it away. Then, "Hey," he said. "You want to see a magic trick?"

"I don't know. Sure."

"Give me something," he said.

I handed him a twig.

"No," he said. "Something that means something to you."

I looked down at the pearl ring on my hand, then up at him.

"Yes," he said. "That."

The ring had been my mother's when she was a child, and her mother's before that. I loved it, and since I'd been given it, I'd never taken it off; I feared misplacing it. But I handed it to Wayne, then covered the newly naked spot with my other fingers, protecting it.

Wayne pulled a small box from his pocket, put the ring inside it. Then he shook it, and I could hear the ring moving about. He opened the box, showed me the ring lying there.

"Okay?" he said.

I nodded.

He closed the box again, began moving it slowly about. "The earth is a strange and wondrous place," he said. "Think of all you can't understand. I mean, even . . . look up at the sky."

I looked at the box. I wanted the ring back.

"No," he said. "Trust me. Look up at the sky."

I looked up.

"How did those stars get there?" he asked.

"God."

He laughed. "Who's God?"

I couldn't believe he had said this. I feared, momentarily, for his life: lightning. A small flood. A boy heart attack, Wayne lying on his stomach, his hands reaching out uselessly, his face purplish blue. I said loudly, "What do you mean who's God, *God* is God." I waited; nothing happened. Well. I had saved us.

I looked again at the box. Wayne shook it and I heard the reassuring rattle of the ring. "Sometimes you see something that isn't there," he said. "And sometimes . . ." He put his hand over the lid of the box. "You *don't* see something that *is* there." He opened the box. It was empty.

I burst into tears, surprising myself. "Give it back!"

"Oh, no," he said, "don't *cry*!"

"I'm not crying."

A moment. I snuffled, wiped at my nose with the back of my hand. "I'm *not*!"

"You want your ring back?"

"Yes."

"Okay. All right." He passed his hand slowly back over the box. "I am calling on all my powers," he said, "to brrrriiiing back the rrriiiing."

He opened the box, and there the ring was. I snatched it up, put it back on my finger, touched it once, twice. Then I asked, "Is this the same one?"

He nodded, lay down, closed his eyes.

I looked carefully. The ring was indeed the same one—there was the bent prong that my mother had said we needed to get fixed.

Now I was glad I'd kissed him; he was amazing; I wanted to kiss him again.

"How'd you do that?" I asked.

"Magic."

"No, really. How did you do it?"

"I can't tell you that, Ginny. It's the magician's code. But I can tell you I did it when you weren't paying attention. That's the first thing you learn, to distract the audience. Have them look away. Patter."

"What's patter?"

"It's all the things you say. You know, you just talk, and people get distracted, they don't see what's happening right in front of them."

"It seems too easy."

"It is easy. You know why?"

"Why?"

"Because people want to be fooled."

I thought about this. I supposed it was true.

I lay down beside him, moved my hand to be closer to his, then closed my eyes, willing him to pick up that hand and hold it. I liked everything about this nearness to a boy, liked the foreign, lemony smell of him, the pitch of his voice, the comb lines in his hair, the blunt cut of his fingernails. Being with him, I was doing so many things I had never done before. I felt a jangly nervousness, as though I were at the starting block of a race going somewhere I knew absolutely nothing about. And yet I also felt at peace. Sure of something.

Wayne looked over at me. "Ginny? I need to tell you something. I want to. Jasmine? She's my mother."

I opened my eyes, stared at him. A clock inside me stopped ticking.

"Her real name is Carol MacAvoy."

"Nuh-huh," I said. *People want to be fooled.*

"Yes. It is. But you can't tell anyone. She's hiding from my father. He's . . . It's better if she's not with him."

"Why?"

"Oh, he . . . won't let her do things. She has to stay in the house. And . . . Well, I've seen him hit her."

"He hits her?"

Wayne nodded.

"You're just kidding, right? You're fooling me."

"I'm not. He doesn't do it all the time. Just sometimes."

"He *hits* her?" I couldn't imagine this. Like a boxer? Like a spanking? I envisioned my mother standing in her apron in the middle of her kitchen, her hand to her reddened cheek, her eyes wide and full of tears. But when I tried to imagine my father hitting her, I couldn't. He would cry, too, should he ever do such a thing.

"But why would he hit her?"

"Oh, he just has this really bad temper, I don't know. He's a very powerful man. Very wealthy. Very powerful. And she just one day ran away, took a bunch of money and left. But she always tells me where she is; she tells one of her friends who tells me. She moves a lot. She won't be here longer than six months or so."

"How long ago did she leave?" I looked closely at him, checking his face for pain. But it was smooth and impassive, plain as a bar of soap.

"Two years now, a little over."

"Does your father know you're with her?"

"No." He smiled. "No, he certainly does not."

"How did you get here without him finding out?"

"Oh . . . Magic."

"No, how?"

"I can't tell you," he said. "I've told you too much already, I shouldn't have said all this. Please don't tell, Ginny. You could really get us in trouble." Now he was not impassive. Now I could see the fear in his face. It made me want to build a house for him, just his size, then stand outside looking in the window at him sitting in his own chair by his own little fireplace. "There," I would tell him. "You see? You're fine."

Something occurred to me. "Why don't you just live with your mother?"

"Ginny. If I did that . . . Look, I can't live with her. And you can't tell anyone what I just said. Not even Sharla. Please."

I sat up, stared straight ahead.

"Ginny?"

"I won't," I said. And I knew I wouldn't.

"Okay," he said. "Forget about all that, all right? Just forget I told you. Let's do something else. Let's get married now. We'll change our names. We'll give ourselves new ones. Mine will be . . . Buffalo Bill Cody."

"I'll be Ave Maria," I said. "Ave Maria Cody."

"Good," Wayne said. "That's nice."

I had once wanted to name a doll Ave Maria, for the undulant beauty of the syllables. Sharla said I could not, that it didn't make sense. I wasn't sure what *sense* "Sharla" or "Ginny" made, but I changed the doll's name to Nancy; then promptly hated it and finally beheaded it, stuffed it in the garbage amid potato peelings and broccoli stalks. It felt good to resurrect an idea I once thought was valuable, to have it so easily accepted by someone.

Wayne stood, then pulled me up beside him, and put his arms around me. "Before all the stars in the heavens, I take you, Ave Maria, for my wife."

I was silent for a long time. Then I said, "Before all the trees in the forest, I take you, Buffalo Bill, for my husband." We kissed. Newly.

"Want to sleep out here with me all night?" he asked.

I didn't know. But now that we were married, I no longer had a choice, did I? I went into the tepee and lay down. Wayne lay next to me, one arm around me. I felt uncomfortable, but I was afraid to move. He was my husband now. This was how we slept. I could tell when Wayne fell asleep: his breathing grew deep and even; and though he remained next to me, I could feel him move away. I felt lonely and my hip hurt from lying on my side so long against the hard ground. I thought of Sharla, loose-limbed and relaxed, her mouth open slightly, dreaming deeply in the bedroom we had shared since I was born. I could feel the gauzy pull of sleep, but I could not relax into it. I was worried about getting caught. I was worried about where my mother was. I wanted a drink of water. I wanted to know that if I had to go to the bathroom, I could. But I stayed in the teepee until the light started to break, waking Wayne up; then we snuck back into our houses.

Sharla's arm hung over the bed, her bracelet showing. I covered it with her sheet, then lay down on my own bed, heavy with secrets.

I awakened with a thin line of pain across my forehead and at the top of my eyes. Sharla was lying on her made bed, reading *American Girl*. "Well, *finally*!" she said, when she saw me sit up.

"What time is it?" My voice was thick, lazy.

"It's not even *mor*ning anymore. I already had lunch."

I scratched my knee, yawned. "What did you have?"

"Pinwheel cookies and some Fritos."

I stopped scratching. "Where's Mom?"

"At the grocery store. She has the Tupperware party tonight. Even though it's her birthday."

"Oh yeah."

"We need to make her a card. And this morning Dad gave us money to buy something—we have to do that this afternoon, Ginny."

"Okay." I hated buying birthday presents with Sharla; I wanted to give my own ideas, free and clear. But this was the way we always did it—our father would give us ten dollars, and we had to agree on something, usually from Monroe's. Last year, in addition to the usual pastel stationery and two embroidered hankies, we had gotten her a limp silk-flower corsage. I'd thought it useless, but in fact my mother often wore it. This year I thought we should get her a magazine subscription of her own to *Good Housekeeping*. Mrs. O'Donnell used to give her her old copies; now my mother's supply had been cut off. But I needed to find a way to have Sharla think it was her idea.

"Only two weeks till *your* birthday," Sharla said.

"I know."

"I got you your present already."

"You did? When?"

"The other day. You didn't know."

I stayed silent, thinking. I had always made it my business to know when people bought my presents.

"You don't pay as much attention as you used to," Sharla said, as though she'd heard my thoughts.

"Yes, I do." My head throbbed. I lay back down.

"I mean to *me*, you don't pay as much attention to me."

"Sharla?"

"What."

"Am I hot?"

"How should I know?"

"No, I mean . . . I feel like I have a fever."

She came to sit beside me, put her hand to my forehead. "You're just tired," she said. "You were out the whole night."

"How do you know?"

"I woke up a lot. You were never here."

Suddenly I remembered my mother, outside in her nightgown. "Sharla, did you see what Mom did last night?"

"When?"

"Last night, out in the backyard, when I was out with Wayne."

"What do you mean? She wasn't outside. She was sleeping before you ever went out there."

"No, she came out, and she was walking around flapping her arms and acting crazy."

"What are you talking about? She didn't do that. You dreamed it."

"I *saw* her, Sharla! Wayne did, too. Ask him!"

"Well, that would be pretty hard to do, since he left this morning."

"What do you mean?"

She shrugged, returned to her magazine. "A car came and picked him up. I saw. He got in with a suitcase. He's gone."

I stood up, then sat back down on my bed. Something inside me felt pulled in two directions, being slowly ripped. "He didn't say anything about leaving. He didn't tell me."

Sharla picked up a peach pit she'd put at the side of her bed, sucked on it with noisy satisfaction. "Well, he's gone."

But I *loved* him, I wanted to say. Of course I did not

say it. The words were too big for my mouth. Everything I had felt—and learned—about Wayne was too big for me, and I knew it. So although the suddenness of his departure made for a caved-in feeling, I also felt a kind of buoyancy of spirit, a return to the safety of the self I knew. I felt the kind of relief you experience when you yank your gaze away from staring too long at something, becoming hypnotized by it; becoming, in fact, nearly lost to it.

Later that day, I went into the teepee to think about things. I saw a rock just inside the entrance, holding down a piece of paper. *Ginny,* it said. *I have to go. You know why. You know everything. Don't forget anything.* At the bottom of the note were two parallel lines within a circle, identical to those we'd drawn in the dirt. I pressed the note to my chest, then against my forehead. I cried a little. Then I brought the note inside and put it away in my secret box. I knew I would never see Wayne again. That note was the only proof I had of having learned something essential: how to be properly loved.

The plane tilts suddenly to the left, then rights itself. Why? I imagine the captain taking his hands off the wheel to stretch, then saying, "Whoops!" But no one else is reacting, at least as far as I can tell.

I close my eyes, rub my temples, think again of Wayne. I wonder what he looks like now. I wonder if he ever thinks of me and our little ceremony. It's hard to imagine it didn't mean something to him, that incredible exchange. I hope it did; it certainly meant a lot to me. I've tried to explain how it felt to a few people, but it always gets reduced to a that-summer-at-the-lake story, and that's not what it was. I don't know quite how I could have believed in so much so soon, how I could have taken such chances. Well, he was a compelling character. Charismatic—Jasmine's son, after all. If he hadn't so abruptly left, I wonder what else I might have done with him.

I suppose in my pied-piper delirium I might have subconsciously been imitating my mother. I've seen things like that in my own daughters, God knows—over and over, I've seen behavior in them that parallels my own, in one way or another. Sometimes I think what you say to kids doesn't make a damn bit of difference. It's all in what you do. It really is. It is all in what you do.

*I*n Monroe's lingerie department, Sharla held a nightgown up before me. It was pale blue, decorated with stiff-looking lace around the neck and armholes. "How about this one?" she asked, but she was not really asking. She was demanding. We'd been looking at things for over an hour, and she was tired of it.

"Fine," I said. I was tired, too. More than that, I felt really sick: dizzy and weak, and my head throbbed.

Sharla paid for the nightgown, then turned to me and said, "Do you want to go and get it gift-wrapped? We have enough."

Her words sounded as though she were speaking underwater. I stared dumbly at her. I would answer her later. After a nap.

"Ginny?" She walked over and put her hand to my forehead. "Uh-oh. Let's go." She started to leave, then looked behind her at me, standing there. "Come on!"

I followed a few steps, then stopped.

Sharla came up beside me, grabbed my arm. "Hurry up!" she hissed. "Do you want everyone to know you're sick?"

Another difficult question. I shrugged, then sat on the floor.

"Will you *stop* that?" Sharla bent down to pull at me.

The package with the nightgown slipped out from under her arm, and I reached for it, uselessly. It was too far away.

The saleswoman who had helped us, a thin, older woman wearing a navy dress with white polka dots, glasses perched at the end of her nose, came over to us. "What happened here?" she asked. "Are you all right?"

"No," I said, vaguely, watching the polka dots swim; but Sharla quickly followed with, "Yes. She's fine. She just fell down a little. We're going." She yanked on my arm again, and I lay down on the floor.

"What's your phone number, girls?" the saleswoman asked.

I closed my eyes. The cool linoleum felt so good against the side of my face. I pulled my knees up to my chest, pushed my fists between my knees. If they would just leave me alone. If they would just pull the shades and tiptoe out now.

From far away, I heard Sharla say the digits to our phone number. "Home," I thought, and the word suggested such richness I thought I could smell it, sweet and buttery.

"It's like syrup," I told Sharla, who was now kneeling at my side, looking around. She was embarrassed; a pretty shade of rose flushed her face.

"What's like syrup?"

"Home." I felt wise and benevolent, forgiven and all-forgiving, and very, very light. I smiled.

A moment, and then Sharla said, "Oh boy, you are really going to get us in trouble. It's Mom's *birth*day!"

I thought this over for a moment, and then closed my

eyes again. I couldn't care. It wasn't that I didn't care; it was that I couldn't.

I felt the weight of something on my mattress and opened my eyes to see my mother sitting there. "Are you better?" she asked. "Do you feel any better?" She was wearing rouge and mascara and red lipstick, a nice blue dress. At first I thought she did it to make me feel better, but then I remembered the Tupperware party.

I blinked, yawned. "I think so."

"You slept well." She put her lips to my forehead. "Your fever is down. It's about a hundred now." My mother had an uncanny ability to estimate fever using her lips alone. She had never yet been off by more than two-tenths of a degree.

She crossed her legs, sighed. "You want some Jell-O?"

"No."

"Ginger ale?"

"No."

She looked at me for a long moment, frightened, I knew; it frightened her when we didn't eat. And so, "What kind of Jell-O?" I asked.

She smiled, relieved. "Cherry, you know how you like that. Would you like me to just bring some up here and leave it?"

I nodded. It would make her feel much better to do that. I could always flush it down the toilet.

The doorbell chimed, and my mother looked at her watch. "Oh, they're here," she said, her voice a mix of pleasure and disappointment. And then, "I'll come up here and check on you, Ginny, but I couldn't cancel the party—it was too late. Sharla will stay with you, she'll be right up." She went out into the hall, called her.

"I'm getting the *door*," Sharla called back, and then I heard her welcoming Mrs. Spurlock in her best company voice.

My mother kissed my forehead. "You just let Sharla know if you need anything."

"Mom?"

"Yes, honey?"

"Happy birthday."

"Oh, never mind about that."

"We got you something."

"Yes, I know. Thank you."

"You'll open it tonight, right?"

She looked again at her watch, smoothed her skirt. "Of course I will. I can't wait." She went out into the hall, called once more for Sharla, who yelled that she was *coming*, though she had not been.

When Sharla finally came into the room, she put a dish of Jell-O on the bedside table, making a point of not looking at me. She walked over to the window, stood silently for a while, staring out. Then she flopped on her bed and turned toward me.

"Well, you went and nearly died right in Monroe's Department Store."

"Not hardly."

"Mary Jo Bennet was there with Francine O'Connell. They walked right past us. I'm sure they saw you there on the floor. They probably thought you were having a fit or something."

I said nothing. I would not apologize for being ill.

Sharla put her pillow over her stomach, shaped it into

a mound. "Look at me, I'm pregnant." Then, pulling the pillow off and throwing it to the floor, she sighed. "Do you want your toenails painted or something?"

"I'm too tired."

"You don't have to *do* anything."

True. "Okay."

Sharla took the red nail polish out of our dresser drawer, shook the bottle. She sat down at the bottom of my bed, legs akimbo, and, using two fingers, lifted my foot by its big toe to put it in front of her. Then she wiped her fingers on the sheet.

"They're *clean*," I said.

"They're your *feet*," she answered.

Then, despite her disgust, she began painting my toenails carefully, her hand shaking a little with the effort. "Mrs. Spurlock had on pearls with her dress," she said. "A pearl necklace *and* a pearl bracelet."

"What color dress?"

"Pink."

"Yeah," I sighed. Pink and pearls. Beautiful.

The doorbell chimed again. I heard Jasmine's voice, followed by several others. They were excited, congratulatory, soothing, confidential. High and female and interesting. The women would be perfumed and wearing high heels and attractive summer dresses in the colors of sherbet and roses. Some of them would have matching sweaters draped over their shoulders. Hair would be styled and sprayed, earrings screwed on straight. Nylon stockings would be shining and making their sandpapery sounds every time the women crossed their legs. I wanted to be down there. I was tired of being sick, now.

"Did you get to taste anything yet?"

"Just some nuts and mints. I'll get the good stuff later."

I waited. Sharla looked up. "Don't worry about it. I'll bring you some, too."

I breathed out, satisfied. I didn't want to eat anything. I just wanted to look at it.

I heard the stairs creak, and then there was Jasmine, standing in our bedroom. Her eyes widened. "Well, look at you," she said. "Sick as a dog on a day like today." She pulled a bag out from behind her back. "I wonder what's in here."

I smiled, scratched lazily at a mosquito bite.

"I just wonder." She looked inside the bag. "Oh, yes. That's a good thing. And oooh, that's good, too."

She handed the bag to Sharla. "Give her something every fifteen or twenty minutes," she said.

"Starting now?"

Jasmine nodded.

Sharla pulled out a *Photoplay*, smiled at the cover, then at Jasmine.

Jasmine smiled back, kissed my forehead like a second mother, left the room.

"She's never been to a Tupperware party," Sharla said, leaning over my foot to finish painting the pinkie.

"Her real name is Carol," I said.

Sharla looked up. "What? I think you're talking crazy again. Do you feel sicker?"

I'd regretted saying what I did as soon as the words were out of my mouth. Now I welcomed this opportunity to escape from them. "Hoola-moola," I said.

"Ginny?"

I rubbed my eyes. "I think I need to sleep."

She groaned, put the top back on the nail polish.
"Well, I have to stay here. Can I read your magazine?"

"Read it out loud."

"But you said you wanted to sleep!"

"I can hear in my sleep."

Sharla moved back onto her bed, stretched out. "Okay,
this is the first story," she said. " 'Where Rock Hudson
goes, girls are sure to follow. And why not?' "

She continued to read aloud in her patient monotone. I
closed my eyes, imagining life in Hollywood.

"Did you hear that?" she asked suddenly.

I opened my eyes.

"They're doing 'Two Things.' "

"Let's go."

I still felt weak, but duty called. Sharla and I tried
never to miss the Two Things part of a Tupperware
party. Next to the sight of the long table, loaded up with
plastic containers for everything imaginable and draped
with a dark tablecloth with "Tupperware Home Parties"
embroidered on it, Two Things was the best part of the
party. It was done as an icebreaker before the demonstra-
tion and sales began: the famous "burp" of air from the
container when you sealed it, thus guaranteeing fresh-
ness of the leftovers; the showcasing of the adorable Pop-
sicle makers, which I wanted desperately but which my
mother refused to buy, calling them an unnecessary ex-
travagance. "We can make Popsicles in juice cans," she
always said, but we never did.

For Two Things, all the women sat in a horseshoe before the display table. Then, at the prompting of the
hostess, each woman said her name and two things
about herself. Sharla and I always had high hopes that

something fantastic would be revealed; nothing ever was. Still, the information was entertaining. Last time, Mrs. Jacobson had revealed that her cat had had seven kittens, named after the seven dwarfs.

We sat at the top of the steps, leaning forward to hear better. Joan Phenning said that her favorite food was brussels sprouts and that she had two beautiful boys. Sharla and I looked at each other. Tweedledee and Tweedledum, that's what we called her two beautiful boys. Mrs. Five Operations said she had reached the six-month mark after her laminectomy and could now lift grocery bags. Also that she had a new recipe for a cold cucumber soup in her purse that she was willing to share with anyone who was interested. My mother said she expected gigantic roses later this summer and that today was her birthday. There ensued a happy chorus of "Ohs!" and "Happy Birthdays!" And then we heard Jasmine say, "My name is Jasmine Johnson. I wanted to be an actress and I never loved my husband." There was a stunned silence. Then a titter, and some rustling sounds. And then, "My name is Jane Samuelson. This summer we're going to Wyoming, and next week my older daughter Janie will be getting her braces off. And—well, I wanted to be a dancer. But that's three." Sharla and I sat immobile. We did not look at each other. The next woman, Eileen Hansen, went back to the usual format, saying what her husband did and how many children she had. After Two Things was over and Sharla and I went back to the bedroom, she asked, "Why does Jasmine *say* things like that?"

"I don't know."

"Sometimes she is so *weird*."

"Yeah."

"Why does Mom *like* her so much?"

I picked up my bowl of Jell-O. "Because she's so different."

"Huh," Sharla said. "That would make someone *not* like her."

"Not everyone," I said. The Jell-O was wonderful. It slid effortlessly down my throat. I wanted more.

My father brought pizza home for my mother's birthday dinner. She'd said she didn't want to leave me to go to a restaurant when I was sick, though I felt much better. "Twelve-hour virus," my father had pronounced, then tousled my hair. "Right? You're better already, right?"

I'd nodded. He didn't like it when anyone was sick: he had to make it into something nearly gone as soon as it arrived. When Sharla was hospitalized for a week with her tonsils, he was beside himself; that was the most serious thing that had happened to us. He called the nursing station relentlessly when visiting hours were over; he held Sharla's hand the whole time he was there with her; he told her as soon as she awakened from anesthesia that she was all better. It was an odd feeling, being sick around him; you felt secure in his assurance that you were fine; but you felt frustrated, too, at the distance between what he said you felt and what the truth really was.

After pizza, served unceremoniously on our usual dinner plates and accompanied by a salad my mother made, my father presented her with a large package, and Sharla put our gift on top of it. She'd used Christmas paper to wrap it; my mother smiled at the sight of flying reindeer in August. "I wanted to get it gift-wrapped,"

Sharla said, "but Ginny got sick." She looked accusingly at me.

"This is fine," my mother said. "More interesting. It's nice to have something unexpected once in a while." She untied the red ribbon. "Let's see what's in here." She took off the paper carefully, folded it. Then she lifted the box cover and held up the nightgown. I looked closely; I'd forgotten what we'd bought.

"Do you like it?" Sharla asked.

"Yes, I do. Very much. Look at this pretty lace trim."

"I mostly picked it, because Ginny was sick."

I opened my mouth to protest, but could think of nothing to say. It was true.

"But I couldn't have done it without her." This seemed extreme, but as I was the beneficiary of Sharla's remark, I let it stand.

"I'll wear this tonight," my mother said.

Next she opened my father's gift to her. It was a set of copper-bottomed pans. "They're beautiful," my mother said. She picked up a smaller, wrapped box that had been put in with the pans. "But what's *this*?" She shook the box, looked at my father out of the corner of her eye. Then, playfully, she asked, "What did you do, Steven?"

"Open it," he said.

It was a can of copper cleaner.

"Oh." My mother smiled, nodded.

"Do you like those pans?" he asked.

"Yes."

"You've always told me how much you love copper-bottomed pans. This is the whole set."

"Yes, it is. Thank you, Steven."

"That's not all, though. That's not all. How about some cake?"

"There's cake?" my mother asked.

"From Schickman's," my father said proudly. He hiked up his pants, smoothed the back of his hair.

"Oh, Steven, you didn't have to go there." Schickman's was the bakery across town; their cakes were delicious, but very expensive.

"It's your birthday," he said. "I love you." Sharla and I looked at each other, smiled.

Our father went into his den, returned with a pink box. He opened it with a flourish. HAPPY 35TH! was written in purple frosting across a large white cake, beautifully decorated with latticework, pink frosting roses, and candied violets.

"What a lovely cake," my mother said. "Of course, it's . . . Well, I'm thirty-six, you know."

My father leaned over the box. "What the—" He stepped back, thought for a minute. Then, "Oh, Marion," he said. He picked up her hand, kissed it. "What must you think of me. Of course it's thirty-six, I know that. I was in such a hurry to get home, I didn't even check at the bakery to see if the thing was right. The girl must have misunderstood me when I phoned in the order."

My mother went to the silverware drawer, returned with a knife. "It's all right. It will taste just fine. It will taste wonderful. I'd rather be thirty-five anyway."

"I'm so sorry," my father said. "I know I told her right."

"It doesn't matter." I looked at the curve of my mother's eyelashes against her cheek as she started to cut into the cake; she was still made up from her Tupperware party, and she looked very pretty.

"Why don't you go out dancing?" I asked.

Both my parents looked at me.

"I'm fine now," I said.

"You want to, Marion?"

My mother laughed.

"Go!" I said. "Or go . . . I don't know, somewhere."

"You want to go out?" my father asked again.

"Well . . . I don't know, maybe we should." She sat down, the knife still in her hand. "Where should we go?" She was happy now, expectant. Beneath the table, I saw her foot reach for the heels she had slid off. I felt proud of myself.

"I don't know. Maybe . . . I don't know. Where do you want to go?"

Her smile froze, then faded.

"You just think of a place," he said, "and I'll take you there."

She looked away, shrugged. "Never mind." Her voice was soft.

"What's wrong?" He crossed over to her, took the knife out of her hand. "Just *think* of a place, Marion, and I'll *take* you!"

She looked up at him. "Why don't *you* think of a place, Steven?"

He stood there. Blinked. "Okay," he said, finally. "Well, let's see. Let's see." He sat down at the table with us, folded his hands before him. We waited. The cuckoo clock sounded, absurdly: it was seven o'clock. I found this sad, somehow; it seemed too early and too late both.

My mother took the knife back from my father, cut

into the cake. She smiled, lips tight. "Let's just eat this, okay? I don't need to go out. I feel better staying home when Ginny's sick." She cut one piece, then another, then another, one more; handed them out. The silence felt draped around us.

Finally, "I'm *better*!" I said, to no one, apparently. Sharla sat still at the table, staring into space, then picked up her fork.

We ate in silence. And then the cake was put in the refrigerator, the thirty-five having been clumsily changed into a thirty-six. My father used a fork to do it. He wasn't careful enough; it didn't really work.

There was one awful year when my husband forgot my birthday. Usually, he would serve me breakfast in bed— that was always one of the best presents. But this year he said nothing about my birthday all day. I wasn't worried. It was a Saturday, and I kept waiting, thinking he had a surprise party planned. The kids didn't mention my birthday either, but that wasn't unusual—they were only four and six. Sharla called that afternoon when Mark was at the hardware store. She asked what he had given me and I said nothing yet, that I thought he had some big surprise planned. Then I asked if she knew what it was. "No," she said, and I could tell she wasn't lying, and it was then that it began to occur to me that he had forgotten. I didn't tell her that, though, nor did I tell my father and Georgia when they called a few minutes later. They, too, asked me what Mark had gotten me. This time I did not smile and say I thought he had something planned. This time I felt like punching them for asking.

Mark remembered right before we went to bed. He

felt terrible. He got dressed and went to an all-night grocery to get a card and a bouquet of flowers, and the next day he served me a spectacular breakfast in bed.

But what happened on my mother's birthday, that was different. It was completely different.

*T*he morning after the Tupperware party, I awakened feeling fine. I left Sharla sleeping and came into the kitchen to see my mother sitting at the kitchen table, a small book before her. "What's that?" I asked.

"It's a book of poetry. By Edna St. Vincent Millay."

"Where'd you get that?"

"Jasmine gave it to me for my birthday. That, and this." She pointed to her neck, and I saw a thin gold chain, holding a locket.

"That's pretty. What's inside?" I knew already: photos of me and Sharla. I couldn't wait to see.

"Nothing, yet." My mother tightened her hand around the locket.

"You can use my school picture," I said. "Part of me would fit."

"Good," she said. "Yes. I'll do that."

I sat opposite her, looked at the book she had open to somewhere in the middle. "Why did Jasmine get you a *poetry* book?"

She looked up. "I love poetry."

"You do?"

"Yes."

"Oh."

167

She got up, went over to the refrigerator. "Do you want scrambled eggs?"

"What's wrong?" I asked. Something was.

"Nothing."

A silence, thick and unrelenting. She stood waiting before the open refrigerator door, her back to me. "I'll just have cereal," I said, finally.

The next morning, our father stayed home from work. "For nothing," he said. "For fun."

He had never done this, and it astounded and delighted Sharla and me. It also frightened us. We looked at our mother for signs of life-threatening illness and found none. We looked at our father, at ourselves. All seemed well: skins were pink; eyes were clear; no one limped or coughed or moaned. All seemed well except that our father was staying home from work. It was like finding two yolks in an egg: a bonus, but an anomaly that made you a bit nervous.

My mother seemed suspicious at first, then guardedly happy. We all sat in the living room in our pajamas, thinking about what we might do. My mother wanted to go on a picnic, but outside thick gray clouds moved restlessly about, as though the sky had been set for a slow boil. It looked like we were in for yet another day of storms.

"It'll clear up by noon," she said. "I'll make some potato salad."

She started potatoes cooking, then went up to dress. By the time she came down, the rain had started. Fat drops splattered against the window, drummed at the gutters; the wind whipped the branches of the bushes and pulled blossoms off the flowers in the garden. She stood at the kitchen sink, looking out the window, immobile.

"Let's have a picnic anyway," my father said.

My mother looked at him.

"Inside, I mean."

"Inside?"

"How about in the living room?" He was dressed in his Saturday clothes: khaki pants, a plaid, short-sleeved shirt open two buttons at the throat. His hands were in his pockets, as though seeking protection behind that thin fabric; he looked to me like a boy asking for his allowance early.

"I don't know about having a picnic inside," my mother said. "What would be the point?"

"Fun!" I said.

She nodded. Did not smile. Although her mouth moved slightly, as if she were trying to.

While she finished making lunch, the rest of us sat at the kitchen table, keeping her company. Sharla and I had a stack of magazines. We were "doing houses," as we called it, cutting out things to put in our piles. If you saw a dress you liked, you put that in there and it was yours, hanging in the closet of your dreams. If you cut out a Cadillac convertible, it was parked in whatever garage you imagined (and Sharla once imagined a garage with a swimming pool in it). Today, I dropped a white cake with cherry-fluff frosting in my pile, then added a hat and coat ensemble, then an entire kitchen. Sharla was concentrating on furniture; thus far, she had a nubby green tweed sofa, a Sylvania television, and a club chair. My father watched us for a while, then took a magazine for himself and began cutting things out. He told us he was going to make a collage. We stopped our own work to watch him: he taped a pair of brown wing tips inside a DeSoto, taped a roast onto a Frigidaire dryer. He found a white picket fence and taped a woman behind it; next to that, he put the face of a fair-haired child looking out of a window.

My mother finished with the ham sandwiches and came over to watch my father, hands on her hips. Then she, too, sat down and began leafing through magazines. She cut out a pair of red high heels. Next she cut out the picture of a small bird, and, with great care, cut his wings off. These she affixed to the heel of the shoes. She stared at her creation, then sat back, her arms crossed.

"What have you got there, Marion?" my father asked.

My mother smiled, shrugged.

"Where are those shoes going?" I asked.

"I don't know."

"Wherever it is, it's fast," my father said.

"Hey, Mom," Sharla said. She held up a picture of an airplane. "Want *this*?"

"Oh, say, *I* could use that," my father said. He reached across the table to take the airplane from Sharla, then asked my mother, "You don't mind?"

"Take it, Steven," she said. Then she sat quietly looking out the window at the storm, which continued to worsen.

When lunch was ready, we assembled ourselves on a quilt before the fireplace. No one talked. We listened instead to the natural symphony of wind and rain, to the reverberation of thunder so loud it seemed it might crack the earth.

By five o'clock that evening, we had lost our electrical power. It seemed to me that this was a real opportunity for a good time, though I was short on specific ideas. But my mother took a flashlight and started upstairs. She said she was going to read for a while, then go to sleep.

"But it's still *day*!" I said.

"I'm tired." She did not turn around to tell me this. I turned angrily to Sharla and my father, who were watching her go up the steps; and in their faces I saw that they each thought it was their fault, too. So I said nothing. Instead, I silently shared the burden.

Sharla and I stayed up until ten, playing Monopoly with our father. The lights had come back on at nine-thirty, for which I was a little sorry. I'd liked seeing the dice roll into shadowy corners of the game board, liked moving my marker with the flashlight ahead of it as though it were a car.

"Are you ever going to play hooky again?" Sharla asked my father.

He took his turn, landed on Chance, pulled a card. "I might," he said. "I'm full of surprises." And then, to me, the banker, "Fifty bucks, please." He showed me the tax rebate card that entitled him to it.

"*You're* not full of surprises." I laughed, handed him the money.

"What do you mean?" He seemed offended.

"Nothing. Just . . . You don't do surprising things. You're . . . regular." My father's routine was unalterable. I could recite the specifics of it to anyone. Every workday morning, he kissed my mother lightly on the lips, kissed the top of Sharla's and my heads; then sang out, "I'll see you at six!" as he was walking out the door. He pulled the car out of the driveway, tooted the horn three times, then proceeded down the street with his hands on the wheel at the ten and two o'clock position. At six in the evening, he did the same thing in reverse: three toots of the horn, a calling out of "I'm home!" as he came in the door, three kisses.

He had a weekend routine, too. And I knew what flavor ice cream he would order when we went out, how and when he wore his slippers, what television shows he never missed, what he would say to his parents when they called. If I asked for a dollar, he'd give me two, admonishing me not to lose them. When he buttered his pancakes, he would cut the pat into four tiny squares before he spread it.

But, "Believe me," he said now, "I can be just as surprising as the next guy."

I thought it was so cute, this lie—it made for a soft spot in my stomach. For him, a man whose habits were so utterly predictable, to say he was full of surprises! I wondered if he actually believed it.

After we went to bed, Sharla and I were talking about what teacher I might get my first year in junior high when our mother came into our room, stood just in the doorway. At first I thought we were in trouble for waking her up. But then she only said softly, "Good-night."

"You slept *all day*!" Now that I knew she was not angry at us, I had the luxury of being angry at her.

"Are you sick?" Sharla asked.

This had not occurred to me.

"No, I'm not sick." She walked over to sit at the foot of my bed, began playing with the thinning tufts on my spread. Then, looking up, she said, "I think I've raised you so wrong."

I held still, the breath inside me feeling like a swallowed balloon.

"What'd *I* do?" I asked, finally.

I could feel Sharla smirking, basking in some unearned victory until my mother said, "No, I mean both of you. You didn't do anything wrong. I did something wrong. I did everything wrong, and I'm sorry." To my horror, she began weeping, her shaking hands covering her face. I had two simultaneous impulses: to embrace her and to shove her.

"Where's Dad?" Sharla asked, her voice barely above a whisper.

My mother waved her hand in dismissal. "Oh—him. Don't . . . This is not . . ." She stood up. "I'm sorry, girls." She kissed my cheek, then Sharla's. "I'm sorry." And then she was gone.

"Dad?" Sharla called softly. And then louder, "Dad?"

He came into the room. His face was drawn, softened by sadness. "Yes?"

"What's wrong with Mom?" Sharla asked. "What's the matter with her?"

I looked down, picked at my thumb. I felt as though my bed were an island, surrounded by a roiling sea. I feared for the rest of my family, but I was fine. I was. I was fine.

I lay down, closed my eyes. "If you want to talk," I said, "go downstairs. I'm going to sleep."

I heard Sharla and my father leave, and I opened my

eyes, lay still and straight in my bed. I could not hear them. I tried, but I could not hear a word.

I turned over, away from the door, raised my arm up to lay my hand flat on the wall as high as I could reach; relished the slight pain caused by the excessive pull of my muscle. Then I received my own arm back to my own self. I wrapped it in the sheet, I kissed it at the wrist, and at the elbow, and then I rocked it.

Then, against my will, I remembered my father coming home from work a few days earlier, walking with gentle fatigue into the kitchen where my mother was making dinner. He'd kissed her, then stood close to her, watching her, watching. He'd turned his hat around and around in his hands, nervously, absentmindedly. My mother had snatched the hat away from him, and the gesture was sudden and violent enough that it had caused her to lose her balance. She'd caught herself against the counter, then handed the hat back to him. "For God's sake, Steven," she'd said. "*Stop* it."

I awakened to the sounds of an argument. My mother was shouting, crying. My father was shouting back. I got out of bed, went into the hall and found Sharla there, sitting at the top of the stairs.

"What are they *doing*?" I asked.

"Shhh!" She patted the floor next to her, and I sat down.

"Even if it *weren't* true, there's other things," my mother said. "There's so much more. You have no idea, Steven. You have no idea! You live your neat life in the way that you want to, you decide everything, you never stop to think about me! As a person, I mean! I'm just . . . your wife. Like your shoes!"

"Marion, I have no idea what you're talking about! When did this *hap*pen? What's the *mat*ter with you? You've never been like this. Never!"

"I *have* been!" she yelled. "I *have* been and *have* been and *have* been!"

"Marion." My father's voice was quiet now.

"No!" she yelled.

A long silence. The grandfather clocked chimed the half hour, then the cuckoo. The wind moved the bushes next to the house and I heard their scratching sound. It used to scare me, that sound. Now it comforted me.

"What do you need?" my father asked, finally. "What should I do?"

Muffled sounds of sobbing.

"Marion. Are you . . . are you having a nervous breakdown?"

She stopped weeping. It seemed as loud as screeching brakes, this sudden quiet.

I heard a chair slide slowly across the floor. "Steven, I am thirty-six years old. I used to tell everyone that by the time I was thirty-five, I would . . . Well, whatever it was I was going to do, it would be done by then. I would have *done* it. But that time has come and gone, and I've done nothing. I am nothing."

"Oh, Marion, don't say that. How can you say that? You're a wife and a mother."

"That is NOTHING!" She yelled this so loud her voice broke, like a boy's when it was changing over into a man's.

I felt a curious combination of anger and pain, a small tornado of emotion twisting up from my stomach into my throat. I took in a breath, gritted my teeth, stood. I was going down there. I was going to present the fact of myself for her reconsideration.

"Don't!" Sharla whispered, and grabbed my arm. She stared straight ahead, unblinking, immobile. Her face was empty of any emotion that I could read.

I jerked away, started downstairs, stopped halfway when I heard my mother say, "I never even *wanted* children! I just *did* it! You had to *do* it, you *had* to do it!"

I leaned against the wall, opened my mouth, closed it.

"But *I* wanted to . . . oh Steven, you just don't know. I'm not like—"

"Marion, I want you to stop this right now. I want you to lower your voice. You'll wake them up. For God's sake!"

I started back upstairs, slowly, slowly. I had two knees, two feet. This is what I thought of. I had two hands, two eyes, two ears. There was a hammer and anvil in the middle ear, I had two of those.

"I don't care if I wake them up," my mother said, but her voice was low now, contrite.

My father sighed. "Do you . . . Would it help to go away? Maybe visit your parents, or . . . just get away?"

A long silence. And then, "Maybe it would."

I saw that Sharla was no longer at the top of the stairs. I went into our bedroom, saw her shadowy C-shape lying in bed, turned away from the door. I got into her bed with her, turned on my side, rested my hand on top of her head. When I used to suck my thumb, I would often hold on to a piece of Sharla's hair, twist it around my fingers. I did this now, lifted a few silky strands of her hair, wound them gently around my pointer. She didn't say a word, just moved over to give me more room. I put my thumb in my mouth, then pulled it out and wiped it on my T-shirt. Then I moved closer to Sharla. We stayed like that.

*I*f Sharla is really, really ill, I'm going to bring her home with me. No one will take care of her like I can. I know that. She knows that, too. No one is closer to her—not her husband, not her children, not our father.

Sometimes I wish so hard that my own daughters would be closer to each other. But it doesn't seem to be happening. They will occasionally work side by side on some project, but they don't look up and exchange things in a glance. They don't seek each other out as playmates or as counsel to each other, at least not yet. A friend of mine once said that she believes it takes some awful adversity to get family members really close—otherwise they only affectionately tolerate each other. She said, "It's kind of like you need Outward Bound at the kitchen table. I mean, every time I find sibs who are really close, it's because they survived something hard together. Don't you find that to be true?"

"I don't know," I said. "I guess I've never really thought about it." Not quite true. Not true at all, actually. I've thought about it a lot. And I think there may be some truth in what my friend is saying. For example, I know the exact moment that Sharla and I moved into a much closer relationship. It was that night when I lay silently beside her, listening to the sad noise of our parents coming apart.

My mother was gone on my birthday. Sharla made me a Duncan Hines white cake with chocolate frosting; she did not know how to make caramel-flavored. My father presented me with gifts he and my mother had gotten earlier: two Nancy Drew books, a very sophisticated chemistry set that I'd wanted for a very long time, stationery featuring the floating trappings of the teenager: telephone, address book, nail polish, rollers, 45s. Sharla gave me a huge-size box of colored pencils and a sketch book. I opened everything with as much enthusiasm as I could muster, then stacked the gifts neatly at the side of the table. Later, I would stack them neatly at the bottom of my closet and drape a pillowcase over the pile.

My father lay between our beds when we went to sleep that night, his arms a pillow behind his head. He kept his eyes closed while he talked. "There's something wrong with your mother right now. But it's temporary. It's strictly temporary. But she's so . . . upset right now, she just forgot it was your birthday, Ginny."

"Oh," I said.

He opened his eyes, looked at me. "It happens, that people can get that upset. It doesn't mean they don't love you. Or that they'll never be right again. It's like . . . you know, a gallbladder operation or something. Remember when Grandma needed her gallbladder out and she was in the hospital? Remember how sick she looked, how she couldn't do anything?"

I nodded, squeezed the edge of my pillow. On a breezy day like we'd had today, my mother often would air the pillows, lay them across the windowsills, half in, half out.

"Well," my father said, "Grandma got better really fast, right? And she came home, and everything was fine. But the whole time she was in the hospital, she forgot about everything that was going on at home."

"Nothing was going on, though," I said. Then at night, the pillows smelled so good. My mother called it God's perfume, that's what she said.

"Well." My father smiled. "You don't know that nothing was going on."

"Not like a birthday or anything," I said. And when my mother did the dishes, she took her wedding rings off and put them on the kitchen windowsill in a little bowl with pink roses on it, that's all that bowl was for. Once, she let me wear the rings, instead of putting them in the bowl. When she had finished the dishes, I held my hand out, giving the rings back to her. "What have you got there?" she asked. I'd thought she was kidding. But she'd forgotten that she'd given them to me.

"I don't think Grandma missed a *birth*day," my father said. "But I'm sure she missed some things."

"Nuh-uh," I said. "She would have told me."

He nodded. "Okay."

"Mom is not in the hospital, Dad," Sharla said. "She is with Jasmine. That is not a hospital."

"She is on a little trip with Jasmine," my father said

carefully. "But she is getting well just the same as if she were in a hospital."

"Yeah, we'll see about *that*," Sharla muttered.

My father sat up. "You really must try to understand, Sharla. Both of you. I know it's hard. But you have to try. She's your mother. She loves you very much, you two are the most important things in the world to her."

We neither of us said anything. But a shared doubt arched up between us.

"We'll have another birthday party for you when she comes home," my father said. "Would you like that?"

I shrugged. No.

"I know she'll feel just terrible when she realizes—"

"She knows!" Sharla said. "She just doesn't *care*! She's not coming *back*, Dad! Why don't you just ad*mit* it?!"

My father went swiftly over to Sharla, put his arms around her. "Oh, honey, you're wrong. You're wrong! This just happens sometimes, people get overwhelmed, they need to get away, they just need . . . *time*! She's coming back. She told me she'd come home in a few days, and she will, I know it."

He had Sharla's head pressed against his chest, and he rocked her with short, jerky little movements. He didn't know how to do it right, how to rock. He didn't have the smooth, dancelike movements my mother did. He was stiff, fighting to keep from crying. His fists were balled, his mouth puckered and trembling.

Sharla was not crying. Sharla's eyes were wide open and unblinking, as cold and flat as a fish's. Some knowledge was inside her that was too big for her; it moved other, familiar things out of the way, killed them. I looked away from both of them, out the window, then up into the black sky, asking a question I couldn't find words for. It came to me that if an airplane flew over us, they would see only the lights coming from our house, the cozy squares of yellow that suggested warmth and safety.

Sharla was right. Our mother did not come back in a few days, or in a few days more. Jasmine's house sat empty; I saw the philodendron on her kitchen windowsill yellow, then wither and die. A light she left on in the bathroom eventually burned out. A few newspapers piled up on her doorstep; then delivery stopped.

Our father had one phone call from our mother, on the day before she was due home. Sharla and I were sitting in the living room, where we had called our father in to watch the evening weather forecast—record highs for heat and humidity were being predicted again, and we all seemed to find the prospect grimly thrilling. When the phone rang, my father answered it reluctantly, but then his face changed. "Your mother," he mouthed, and gestured for us to leave the room, to give him some privacy.

We went as far as the kitchen table and sat there in silence, both of us waiting to talk to her, I was sure, though Sharla would never have admitted it. At one point I made the foolish error of going upstairs to comb my hair, and when I returned to the kitchen Sharla said, "What did you do that for? Do you think she can see you? Do you think she even cares?"

"I didn't do it for *her*," I said. But of course I had.

As it happened, our mother did not ask to speak to either of us. After a long, low-voiced conversation, our father called Sharla and me back into the living room and reported only that our mother would be taking longer than she'd thought to come home. He stared out the window, immobile but for the giveaway movements of his breathing. I watched the hung-up phone, wondering if, wherever she was, my mother was doing the same. Sharla sighed, sank into the sofa, studied her nails with cool blue anger.

Finally, "When *will* she be back, then?" I asked my father.

He shrugged. "I don't know."

"Didn't she say, at all?"

"She said she didn't know."

"Well. . . . Can we write to her?" It occurred to me that this would be better than talking to her on the phone, anyway. What I needed from my mother was private. She knew that, too. That was why she hadn't asked to speak to me. "Dad? Can we write to her?" I asked again.

He turned around slowly, looked at me as though he were considering the miracle of my being, as though I were standing there with a message that could save his life. I mean that the look on his face was one of extreme hope and desperation mixed, and I wanted it to be directed anywhere but at me. I had an impulse to wave my hands, to stamp my foot, and snap my fingers in his face. But then something lifted; he straightened to his full height and moved back into himself.

"Yes, you can write to her," he said. "Of course you can. I just don't know yet where to mail anything. She's . . . traveling around. Deciding where she'd like to stay for a while. But you go ahead and write. She'll like your letters, whenever she gets them. Even if she reads them when she gets home, she'll like them."

"Well, *I'm* not writing her," Sharla said. "I hate her. She's crazy."

"Sharla!" my father said sharply. But when she answered *"What?"* he did not say anything more. He put his hand to Sharla's cheek, swallowed so hugely we all heard it. And then he walked away, went into the kitchen to make dinner.

We were eating much later these days—seven o'clock, even eight. Our father would come home from work and cook in his good clothes, his white shirtsleeves rolled up to his elbows, a dishcloth tucked into the waistband of his pants. Tonight we were having steak again. Steak, baked potatoes, canned tomatoes, canned green beans, and very little conversation around our small table, that's what we would be having. Sometimes he stopped at the bakery for dessert: half a cake. Butter cookies in the shape of leaves, in pastel colors of greens, yellows, and pinks. Sometimes Mrs. Five Operations would stop by with a pie, but it was only so she could gawk; eventually, we stopped answering the door when she came. Other neighbors seemed not to know what to do; they waved from their driveways, smiled tight smiles, and that was all. My father kept a pad by the phone on which to write down messages for my mother; by the time she had been gone for a week, they decreased dramatically. I stopped attending dance school; Sharla told the piano teacher not to come anymore.

We did not go anywhere, Sharla and I. We were ashamed to be seen. We spent days when my father was at work sitting in the backyard making daisy chains;

pulling up fat blades of grass and sucking at their whitened ends; lying on the old quilt and charting the progress of the indifferent clouds across the sky. And we talked. By tacit agreement, we did not talk about our mother. We had become interested in ancient Egypt, and we talked mostly about that. We also looked in the woods for dead squirrels. We were going to try to preserve them, to mummify them. I believe we were both relieved not to find any. At night, we watched television with our father, or lay in bed to read books we found in the living-room bookcase: *Reader's Digest* condensations, mostly.

One day a couple of weeks after our mother left, I went into the house to make Sharla's and my lunch. It was my turn; I was going to make peanut-butter-and-fluff-marshmallow sandwiches and cut them into sliver-thin pieces. I took out the supplies, began making the sandwiches, and then stopped. I'd heard something upstairs, a woman's voice, I was sure of it. "Mom?" I said. A rich silence, the air around me pleated with possibilities.

I started upstairs. My chest was tight with anticipation; I pressed my fist against my sternum. I walked slowly down the hall toward my mother's bedroom, stopped just outside her open door. There were her bottles of perfume, grouped like gossiping friends on her dresser. There was the silver hairbrush her grandmother had given her, the framed photographs of Sharla and me, dusty now. I went over to her closet, yanked the door wide open. If she was in there, I would yell at her. I would not show her any respect. I would hit her, too, as hard as I could.

There was nothing but her clothes and the faint, faint

smell of powder. I pushed my way to the back of the closet, moved some high heels out of the way, and sat down. I took in a huge, shuddering breath. Directly before me hung her green knit dress, my favorite. I squeezed the hem of it in my hand, and began to weep. I cried from deep in my belly for a long time, wiped the tears from my face with her knit dress, then her flowered one, then her brown skirt, then her matching cardigan sweater. And then I went downstairs and made the sandwiches and brought them outside.

"Well, it *took* you long enough," Sharla said. We had a rule that the one making lunch was entitled to absolute privacy, so that no culinary inspiration would be compromised. "Why did you cut them into so many pieces?" she asked. "This is weird. You can't even eat it." She did, though; she put together a few slices and crammed them in her mouth.

"You're supposed to eat them one by one," I said. "It's more delicate. You taste it more."

Sharla looked closely at me. "Were you *crying*?"

I shook my head.

"*Were* you?"

"No."

"Because she's not worth it, you know. She's an ass-a-hole-a."

I sat immobile, trying to make sense of the feel of the sun on my back. Finally, I said softly, "Yeah."

"She's a whore, too."

"She's a fuck," I said, and Sharla's eyes widened. Then she laughed loudly, and so did I.

"Fuck*er*," Sharla said. "She's a fucker and a penis and a vagina. And a shit." We laughed again. It hurt a bit, this reckless laughing; I enjoyed the ache of pain in my stomach. Finally, I sat up, wiped my eyes, and finished my sandwich. Then I went in the house and made another one and ate it. And then one more.

One night at dinner when my older daughter was around ten years old, she ate four servings of strawberry shortcake. I didn't say anything when she did it, or immediately afterward. But when I went into her room to say goodnight, I sat on her bed and asked if there was anything bothering her.

"No," she said.

"Are you sure?"

"Yeah!"

"Okay." I kissed her forehead. Then I said, "You *can* tell me anything. You know that, right?"

"What's wrong with you?" she asked.

"With me? Nothing!"

"Well, why do you think there's something wrong with *me*?"

I busied myself straightening her bedspread. "I don't know," I said. "I just thought . . . well, I noticed you had a lot of dessert. Much more than you usually have. And I do that when I'm upset; when something's bothering me, I eat a lot."

"I just like strawberry shortcake!"

"Okay."

"God, Mom!"

"Okay, I'm *sorry*!"

She looked at me for a while, then said, "I'm your daughter, not you."

"I know."

She raised one eyebrow, something she's been able to do from the time she was a very little girl. "You keep forgetting," she said.

"I suppose." I smiled. Actually, the problem was that I keep remembering.

The Saturday before school started, my father called Sharla and me into his bedroom. He had just awakened—his hair was mussed, his face looked charcoal-smudged with whiskers. "I thought we'd go out for some clothes and supplies today," he said. "For school." A smile. Fake.

"We don't get supplies until after school starts," I said. "The teachers have to tell us what to buy." I hated his not knowing this. I hated his not being fully dressed and competently serving us breakfast before he broached this topic. The way he was doing it was not how it was done. On the day you went shopping for school, you were served breakfast and the shopping plans were laid— where to go, where to go first. After the dishes were done, you were on your way. With your mother. Your mother drove, your mother waited outside the changing rooms while you put together skirts and sweaters, your mother bought your underwear—not your father. I didn't want to be seen with my father, shopping for school clothes. It was dumb. And so I said, "I don't need anything."

"Me neither," Sharla said.

My father blinked, gently rubbed his knee. "But you must need *some*thing."

"We don't," Sharla said.

"We got enough last year," I added.

"It still fits?"

I had no idea. But "Yes," I said. "It still fits. We're fine."

You went shopping with your mother and then she helped you put everything away and then she went and made dinner while you did whatever you wanted and then your father came home and after dinner your mother showed him what you'd gotten. I knew how to do what I needed to live my life. I didn't want to confuse things by doing them another way. It would only be wrong.

Still, my father tried once more to get us to go shopping. After breakfast he said, "You must at least need some pencils and paper."

"Not the first day," we answered together. It was true. Sort of.

"A lunch box?" he asked.

We rolled our eyes, both of us, and he nodded, relieved, in a way.

On the first day of school, I got my period. *That* was something, telling him rather than my mother. Asking him to get what I needed. That, perhaps more than anything, showed me how different things really were now. Say you walked into your own familiar house and the floor gave away beneath your feet. That would be close to what I felt. And tried to pretend I was not feeling. I mean, I just kept trying to walk where there was nothing to walk on. We all did.

* * *

On the third of November, we came home from school and found our mother sitting in our bedroom. I came into the room first, and I nearly screamed when I saw her. I did not, at first, quite recognize her. She had cut her hair into a feathered, caplike do, and she wore blue jeans and a plaid shirt with the sleeves rolled up, something I'd never seen her in before. A red scarf was tied in her hair; the tails hung down past her collarbone.

"You scared me," I said.

She held out her arms, smiled.

"You *scared* me," I said again.

I heard Sharla on the steps, then felt her presence behind me. "What are *you* . . ." she started, and then simply turned and went back downstairs.

My mother lowered her arms, sat quietly.

"No," I said.

"What?"

"No!"

" 'No,' what, Ginny? Come here, for God's sake." She patted the bed beside her.

"Where's Dad?" I asked.

She waited a long moment. Then, "I don't know. At work, I expect. Isn't he at work?"

"He quit," I said. I loved this lie; it was better than a square of Hershey's chocolate melting in my mouth.

She looked at me, said nothing. And then, "No, he did not," she said.

"Uh-huh, he did so. He has a new job."

"And what is that?"

"Administrator," I said.

"Administrator! Where? Of what?"

"What are you doing here?" I asked. "How come you didn't say you were coming? Where have you been?"

"Come *here*," she said gently, and, hating myself, I went and let her hold me.

We sat in silence for a long while. I breathed in the familiar flesh smell of her, watched the shadows of leaves move in the small square of sunlight that came through the window and landed on her knee. At one point, I traced around the outline of that square, gently, wanting her not to move.

And she did not. She merely said, in a voice that let me know she was smiling, "You know what you once called sunlight?"

"No."

"Sun night."

I looked up at her. "Really?"

She nodded. "It was apt, really. You were a couple months short of two, and I was holding you in front of your window—right over there—before I put you to bed. I was swaying just a little, you used to really like that. There was a magnificent sunset that night. And you took your thumb out of your mouth and pointed out the window and said, 'Sun night. 'Night, 'night.' "

I smiled, adoring my baby self.

"And you know what you used to call orange juice?"

I shook my head.

"Undies."

I laughed.

"Yes, you did. And the best—"

"What do you think you're doing?" Sharla asked.

We hadn't heard her come up, but there she was, standing in the doorway.

"Sharla," my mother said, her voice low and soft.

Sharla stood immobile. I pulled away from my mother, moved down a bit on the bed. There was room for us all. Our mother was home now. She would repair everything in the way she always had: sunburned shoulders, saggy hems, darts to the heart from the careless ways of friends.

"Who told you you could come in here?" Sharla asked.

I laughed, involuntarily. That Sharla would suggest our mother needed permission to come into our bedroom!

And yet, "Well . . . no one," my mother said, her voice small and culpable. I hated her acquiescing in this way. Why didn't she take Sharla to task for her rude behavior?

"She can come in here," I said.

"Not on my side, she can't." Sharla breezed over to her bed. She put a glass of milk down on the nightstand, omitting the coaster we were always supposed to use. I waited for my mother to say something. She did not.

"You need a coaster," I said, but before the words were fully out of my mouth, Sharla said, "Shut *up*, baby! You *baby*!"

"Now, just a minute," my mother began, and Sharla whirled ferociously toward her. "You shut up, too! You're not allowed. You're not *allowed*!"

There was a moment of thick, awful silence, and then Sharla started kicking at the air. "Get out!" she yelled. "Just stay out! You're gone! So go!"

I knew she wanted to cry; I could hear the tears in her voice fighting for release, but she would not give in, she would not.

My mother moved to Sharla's bedside. Sharla raised a

fist, then held it, trembling slightly, in the air between them. My mother wrapped her own hands around it. "I know you're angry," she said gently. "I don't blame you."

"I'M NOT ANGRY!"

Well.

My mother let go of Sharla's fist, sat down beside her, then patted the bed on the other side of her. "Come over here, Ginny," she said. And then, to Sharla, "Is it all right if Ginny sits here?" The question came too late; I was already there.

"Yeah, *she* can," Sharla said. "*She* is my sister. You are no one."

My mother sighed, looked away, then down at her feet. I saw that she was wearing tennis shoes and bobby socks. I thought, in some distant portion of my brain, that it looked cute—both bows tied so evenly. In a more distant part I was thinking, I have so much homework. And in the farthest recess, I held the image of my father, standing straight, smiling pleasantly, saying, "Marion? Marion?"

"I would like to tell you girls something," my mother began.

"Sorry, no time to listen," Sharla said, and my mother said sharply, "Stop it, now, Sharla. You *stop* this. I want to tell you something. It's important."

To my surprise, Sharla said nothing.

Our mother rose, crossed over to my bed, and sat down opposite us. Then she looked at us with such aching love I felt the need to shudder, though I did not.

"This is what happened," she said. "I want you both

to know everything. Why I went away. I think it will help you. Okay?"

Sharla said nothing. I nodded, swallowed. I wasn't sure I needed to hear it. I needed only for her to change clothes and start dinner.

Our mother massaged one of her hands with the other, then rested them both in her lap. She cleared her throat, sat up straighter. "You know, I used to shop for groceries on Wednesday night," she said.

At this odd beginning, I knew Sharla and I both wanted to look at each other. But we stayed focused on her.

"Well, one of those nights, early last spring, something happened. I was—"

Sharla belched long and loud with her mouth wide open, then reached for her milk and took a slurpy drink. I wanted to knock the glass out of her hand.

My mother looked at her, said nothing for a long time. I felt the air around us change, felt it grow heavy and specific. Finally, our mother said, "If you don't want to hear this, Sharla, I can't make you. I think it's important for you to listen. For you and for me. But you don't have to. If you would like, I will take Ginny downstairs and talk to her there."

My stomach felt punched. "I—" I began. I didn't know what I wanted to say. I wanted only that my loyalty not be tested in either direction.

But then Sharla spoke. "So *talk*, then," she told my mother. "Go ahead."

My mother took a deep breath, resettled her shoulders. "All right. I went grocery shopping that night and when I was driving home, I passed that place by the river where you can pull over."

"Kids park there," Sharla said.

"Yes, they do," my mother said, and I was shocked that she knew this. "But no one was there that night. And I just wanted to look at the water. I just wanted to be there. I turned off the engine and I sat there for a long time and then I . . . Well, I took my wedding rings off and threw them out the window."

I stopped breathing. My foot, turned for a moment on its side, stayed there.

"I got out right away and found them," she said. "But I didn't put them on. I felt like I couldn't put them back on."

"Why *not*?" Sharla asked, and it irked me that she seemed to know more about this story than what was being told.

And so "Why not?" I asked, too.

She smiled, a sad thing. "I just couldn't. And then I didn't know what to do with them. So I put them in my wallet. And I put my wallet back in my purse and put my purse on the floor. I felt like when you put a baby down, when you're so tired, and you just want to put the baby down, but then when you do, it reaches up for you. And you can't move. You can't lift it again, but you can't walk away, either. You feel . . . stuck. You feel like crying. You feel like screaming. And you feel bad that you feel that way, you feel so *bad*!" She laughed, looked at us as though we might have some idea what she was talking about.

"Anyway, that night, after I put my purse down, I . . .

well, this is really true. I thought I heard the rings talking to me! I thought I heard them whisper. I thought I heard them cry. And so I put them back on."

I smiled, uneasily. She used to try to make up bedtime stories to tell us, sometimes, when we were all done with the library books we'd checked out that week. She would make up stories that were not very good, as this one was not.

But now she was staring at the wall, warming to her own revelations. "I took the rings off because at the grocery store they'd been out of green peppers and I'd started crying. And I knew it wasn't green peppers I was crying about, it was my marriage." She looked at us, shrugged.

"We can't hear this," Sharla said, standing suddenly. "What do you think we are, your *friends*?"

"Can you be?" she asked.

I looked at Sharla for the answer, found it in the line of her clenched jaw.

"You're our mom," I said quietly.

"I'm your mother, but I'm also a person. I'm a *person*!"

"I'm calling Dad," Sharla said, and started to leave the room.

My mother grabbed her arm. "Don't," she said. "Let me finish. Then I'll leave. I'm not staying."

I felt as though one step away from me the earth had opened up wide.

"What do you mean?" I managed. "You just got back. You were gone so long. You just got *back*!"

"Listen to me," she said. "Both of you. You might not

understand everything I'm saying to you now. But you've got to hear it. I can't stay here. I can't be married to your father. In this time away, I have begun to see so much. And I can't be your mother in the old way anymore. I want to be better than that!"

"But you're a good mother," I said quickly, and Sharla just as quickly said, "No, she's not."

"Well you're absolutely right, Sharla," my mother said. "I wasn't a good mother. But I intend to be one from now on."

Sharla snorted.

"Just listen to me," she said. "Let me finish. At the river that night, I got out of the car and I lay down on the ground."

I saw her doing it: she would have smoothed her skirt beneath her, kept her knees and ankles pressed together.

"The trees looked like negatives, I remember that, the leaves weren't out fully, and it was cold, but I didn't feel cold. The moon was full and so beautiful and I remember thinking I wanted it *in* me, to shine *out* of me, you know? To shine out from between my teeth and out of my ears and . . . oh, I just wanted *every*thing to finally *come*!"

"I'm calling Dad," Sharla said again, and left the room. And then she stuck her head back in to say, "Don't stay here with her, Ginny. She's crazy. Come with me. Come on. I'm calling Dad."

I sat still, and Sharla left, clattered down the stairs.

My mother looked over at me. "Do you understand, honey? I felt full of magic for a moment. I felt that anything could happen. Things could really change! And then that feeling all drained out of me. And I got back in the car and I came home. And I put the groceries away. And your father came into the kitchen to ask if I'd gotten baloney and of course I'd gotten baloney because I always got baloney, I brought home the exact same kind and the exact same amount every week. I wanted to take his face between my hands and say . . . and say '*Please*, can we just stop living this lifeless life, can we just let each other out of this prison we've created! I just wanted to—"

I snuffled loudly, involuntarily. I had started to cry and the tears flowed unimpeded down my face, onto my sweater.

"Oh, Ginny," my mother said softly, and she knelt before me, took my hands into hers. "If I stay here, I'll die, I really believe that. We'll be together soon, you and Sharla and I. I'll come and get you. I'll be back. Okay?"

I opened my mouth, took in a jerky gulp of air.

"Ginny, can you possibly understand? I feel I am finally telling the truth."

Something interesting happened then; I watched it from above. Some switch got thrown and I did not care about anything happening before me. Outside, it was growing dark; my father would be coming home soon and we would resume our lives without her. He had learned to make angel cake; we could have it whenever we wanted. He put away clean laundry in our dresser drawers, only rarely making his tender little mistakes.

I started unloading my school books. "I have to do my homework now," I said.

"Ginny," my mother said. "Listen to me. I'm living with Jasmine, she and I—"

Jasmine! "I have so much *his*tory," I said. "My teacher, Mr. Stoltz, he's nuts. He thinks all we have in our lives is *his*tory."

"I am living in New Mexico," my mother said. "I have started art classes, my painting is becoming so . . . I . . . Ginny, don't you see that it breaks my heart not to be living with you and Sharla? But I have finally begun to learn a kind of happiness that I thought I would never know! I have to get stronger in all this, I need to—"

"I want you to go now, please," I said.

Sharla came up the stairs, went over to her bed, dumped her books out of her bag. "Get out," she said, her voice deadly calm. "We don't need you."

I lay down, opened my history book, held it before my face.

I heard my mother start for the bedroom door. "I'll write to you then," she said. "I'll try to tell you in a letter."

"Good-BYYYYYYE," Sharla said.

My mother leaned down to embrace me. She was crying, quietly; I hugged her without looking at her. Then she started toward Sharla, who looked up and said, "If you get near me, I'll call the cops. I swear to God."

My mother touched Sharla's shoe, then left. I heard a car door slam, and I asked, "Did she drive here?"

"Who?" Sharla said.

"Mom."

"Who?" she asked again.

"Mom!" I answered, and then I understood. We did homework for twenty minutes in complete silence, until our father got home. Then we went downstairs to meet him.

"Where is she?" he asked, taking his coat off.

And we told him. Gone again.

Only an hour left before we land. I pull my compact out of my purse, check my makeup, apply some lipstick. Then, staring at my face, I think about the fact that I am older than my mother was when I saw her last. I wonder what she looks like now.

The most recent photographs we have of our mother show her at thirty-five. The last time I looked at those photos was a few Thanksgivings ago, when Sharla and I had brought our families to our father's house for the holiday. The men were watching football, the children playing in the newly installed rec room in the basement. Dinner was running a bit behind, and Georgia insisted she didn't want any help, that at times like this she functioned better alone.

Sharla and I were up in our old bedroom talking about cars; her husband wanted to buy a classic, a blue-and-white '55 Chevrolet. I said I thought that's what we used to have, and Sharla said she thought we had a DeSoto. I said no, I was sure it was a Chevrolet. We went into the attic to get the scrapbooks to check—somewhere in there were pictures with the car in the background.

We settled down next to a big cardboard box full of scrapbooks, dug through photos of Sharla and me with our children, at our weddings, at our college graduations, at our high-school graduations. Finally we reached the period we were looking for and found photos of the car—I was right, it was a Chevrolet. We also found pictures of our mother, which we looked at together. We said very little about them, then or afterward.

I remember Sharla looked at one picture of our family taken by some grandparent or another. It was Thanksgiving, 1955, so many years ago. She looked at it for a long time. Then she passed it to me, saying, her voice a bit thick, "Huh. I guess she was really beautiful, wasn't she?"

I looked at the picture, at the old monogrammed tablecloth, the sparkling dishes, the huge turkey, my father's smile, Sharla's and my neat braids—then, finally, at our mother. And she was beautiful.

"I didn't notice, then, how pretty she was," Sharla said. She was speaking quietly, as though we were in a chapel.

"Kids don't." I looked at the photo again, then said, "But look at *how* she's sitting."

"What? You mean at the end of the line?"

Our mother was seated at the end of the four of us. First came me, then Sharla, then our father, then our mother.

"No, I mean look how far away from the rest of us she is." While the rest of us were touching shoulders, there were a good six inches between my father and my mother.

We looked again at the other photos. Whenever my mother was with Sharla or me, or both of us together, she was close to us, touching us. When it was the whole family, or just her and my father, there was that distance.

There is one movie of our family around that time. It was taken by a man who worked with my father, Joe Valsalvez. He'd bought a movie camera, was thrilled with it, and volunteered to film our family as a gift to my father. The footage of my mother shows her at the kitchen sink. Joe had crept up on her—I remember we all snuck up with him. In the film, she jumps, turns quickly toward us, then starts smiling and wiping at her face. "Onions," she mouths, pointing into the sink. I remember she was answering my father, who had asked, with some embarrassment, why she was crying.

I remember Joe saying loudly, "Oh yeah, my wife, she peels onions, we got a flood! You gotta get a *boat* to get her out of the kitchen!"

I remember something else. It was not onions she was peeling. It was apples, for a pie. I had been in the kitchen with her shortly before Joe started filming. I had seen. We watched that movie only once, borrowed Joe's equipment to do it. The black-and-white images rolled by, you heard the hum from the projector, the tiny clicks of the reel turning. You saw the dust moats float in the steady beam that was directed toward the screen. You saw my mother wipe her face with her apron, smile, and lie. I never called her on it, either. Not then.

*I*n December, a month after we'd last seen her, our mother called around eight o'clock in the evening to tell us she was back in town. She spoke to all of us: first my father, then Sharla, then me. She was living alone in an apartment on Bradley Street, about three miles away from our house. Sharla and I often biked down that street; we thought it was populated only by old people; thought, in fact, that being old was a prerequisite for living there, since we had never seen any other kind of person for the entire three blocks that the street ran. We had always liked watching the residents: women in saggy-bosomed housedresses and loose-weave cardigans; men in pants that fit like elephant skin, their shirts buttoned up to the top, even on the warmest days. We made up lives for them: she was a former beauty queen who became an alcoholic; he was a banker who had lived in a mansion with ghosts.

You could see Bradley Street residents climbing slowly up their outside steps, carrying net bags with miniature loads of groceries: soup, Lipton tea, cans of tuna. You could see them marching purposefully down the sidewalk for their daily "constitutionals," their canes tapping. In the winter, they sat before their front-room windows in dark upholstered armchairs beside equally dark draperies, watching for action on the street; in the summer, they came out to sit on their little screened porches and drink lemonade from tall, sweating glasses. Sometimes, especially when Sharla and I were younger, we would stop and talk for a while, sit cross-legged on this porch floor or that and share with the old folks the uninteresting cookies they seemed to favor.

I could not imagine my mother living on that street, but when it was my turn to talk to her, she assured me she was. "But *where*?" I asked, thinking I must have missed seeing something on that street, some dwelling that might more accurately represent her.

"Number forty-six," she said. "Right in the middle of the block. It's the building that always has red tulips in front every spring."

"Oh," I said.

"You know which one I mean?"

"Yes." I couldn't understand what was she doing there, why she was in that apartment and not in her house. And yet I did not exactly want her home anymore. I did not miss her in the old way: what had felt raw and urgent had changed into something dull and distant—and protected, like the soft essence of a mussel. In many ways she felt less like my mother than some faraway relative whose rare visits brought mostly a guilty discomfort.

I pulled at the phone cord, jiggled my foot restlessly, turned around to look for Sharla or my father. They had left the room.

"Will you come and see me tomorrow?" my mother asked.

I had no idea what to say. I wondered if she had

asked my father and my sister, too, wondered what they had said.

Finally, "I don't know," I said.

"You don't *know*?"

"No."

"Well. Why don't you think about it, all right? I'd like you and Sharla to come over after school. Just for a bit. So we can talk."

I said nothing.

"Ginny?"

"Yeah?"

"Did you hear me?"

"I have to go," I said.

She sighed. "All right. Put your father back on, will you?"

I laid the phone down, called him. He came into the room and picked up the receiver, but did not speak right away. Instead, he looked at me, trying to assess the expression on my face. I made myself crack the smallest of smiles to tell him I was all right. At that point he said hello, but he was still not present to my mother—I heard it in his voice: his mild, floating syllables, his ultimate disregard. He might have been talking to someone soliciting a subscription to an unwanted magazine.

I remembered him sweeping up a broken glass in the kitchen the day before, funneling the shards into the dustpan while his face was raised toward me, talking. The damage was forgotten before it was gone. I remembered, too, his receiving a phone call from a pleasant-voiced woman last night, and how content he had seemed afterward. "Who was that?" I'd asked. He'd put his hand on top of my head, tousled my hair lightly. "Friend," he'd said, in a playful whisper.

I went to find Sharla.

She was standing in our bedroom, looking out the window, her hands in her back pockets. When I came in, she turned around and spoke angrily. "We *have* to go and see her, can you believe that?"

"Who said?"

"Dad."

Actually, I was relieved.

I had read the first few letters my mother sent almost daily; then I began throwing them away unopened. They made no sense to me, what with their talk about her soul, her "growth," the light of truth. And they frightened me. I wanted to relax into a new life that was working out well enough and that did not include her. Our father had lost the pain and bewilderment in his eyes; last Saturday, he had hummed the whole time he made breakfast, and he had made French toast, which he served with strawberries. Yet now I wanted very much to see my mother. It felt programmed into me, a reflex as unstoppable as a blink.

"We'll be together when we see her," I told Sharla. But it was more a question than a statement.

"Of course!" Sharla said. "Do you think he'd let us see her alone? She's dangerous!"

I sat on my bed, scratched at the side of my neck, considered this. My mother had picked out the bedspread I was sitting on. I tried to envision her doing this, standing in Monroe's and sorting through the selections, her pocketbook dangling from her arm. When a figure came into focus, I realized I was not seeing the woman who had last been in my bedroom, begging me to try to understand something. I was seeing someone else, someone who had disappeared from my life as surely as if she had drowned. At that moment, I understood that the person who had so carefully deliberated over this bedspread was never coming back; she was, for all intents and purposes, dead. I shivered, pulled my covers down, and got under them without removing my shoes. Sharla watched me, didn't say a word. Which meant, I decided, that she knew exactly what I was thinking. And agreed.

"It smells like *pee* in here," Sharla whispered. It was six-thirty in the evening; we were in the hallway of our mother's apartment building. Our father had dropped us off, telling us he'd be back in an hour.

"That's not pee," I said.

"Cat pee, I mean."

"It's not cat pee, either. It's medicine."

"How do you know?" Sharla scoffed.

"I just do. It's Vicks VapoRub."

Sharla sniffed the air again. "Oh. Right. I hate that smell."

I didn't. My mother was a great believer in Vicks. Whenever we had colds, she would slather it on our chests at night. I grew to love the smell of it, even the stickiness, believing that it was a cure made manifest: so long as my pajama top adhered to my chest, something was working hard to bring me back to normal.

"What number is it again?" Sharla asked, but the answer was unnecessary; at that moment, our mother opened a door a few feet away.

She was dressed in one of her housedresses, the lemon

yellow one, freshly ironed and stiff at the collar. Her hair was neatly styled; she wore red lipstick and small gold earrings. But her hands were clasped too tightly and she bit absentmindedly at her lip: she was not really put together at all. And when we got closer, I could see that her eyes were red-rimmed; she'd been crying. This annoyed me. Why did we have to come over if all she was going to do was cry?

She embraced me, then Sharla, then gestured toward her open door, saying, "Go right in." And then quickly, laughing, "Well, I hardly need to say that, do I? This is your place, too."

I felt my mouth open in outraged wonder. But I closed it again, said nothing. I didn't have to, because Sharla said loudly, "What are you *talking* about?"

My mother put her finger to her lips, closed the door, leaned against it. "I just mean"—she smiled, waved her arm vaguely toward the small apartment—"that you are as welcome here as in your own house. It really is your place, too."

Silence.

"Well," she said, finally. "Come with me, let me show you something."

Our mother led us down a small, dark hall to a bedroom at the back of the apartment. There were two twin beds there, with barely enough room to walk between them. There was a small dresser, leaning slightly to the left, but decorated beautifully with painted flowers. A small lamp was on the dresser, turned on, and the effect was cozy. On the wall was a small canvas, a painting of a chair in front of a window. It reminded me of the chair my mother sat in at home, but this chair had an ethereal glow, and in the window behind, winding around the wooden rails of a balcony, were flowers the likes of which I'd never seen: shapes like stars, like shells from the ocean. The leaves were veined with thread-thin lines the color of blood.

"Did you paint that?" I asked, my voice a tight bundle in my throat. But I already knew the answer.

"Yes," she said. "And the dresser, too." Then, more tentatively, "Do you like it?"

I shrugged. "I guess. What is that a painting of, anyway? Where is it?"

"It's in my head," she said. "My imagination."

"We're not going to sleep here," Sharla said, suddenly.

"Well, not tonight," my mother said.

"Not ever."

My mother turned toward Sharla. "It's just *here*," she said. "I just wanted to show you that. You have a room here." They stared at each other, neither softening. Finally, my mother said, "Now I'll show you the rest of the place."

"We saw it," Sharla said. It was true: the place was small; we had seen everything on the way to our bedroom. Still, my mother led us on a determined tour. "This is the bathroom," she said. I nodded. Sharla, still angry, would not look at the rag rug on the floor, the pink shower curtain, the bar of Ivory soap emitting the comforting, familiar smell.

"My bedroom," she said, turning on the light and standing aside. It was smaller than ours, I saw; there was room for only a bed and small nightstand. There were books piled on top of the nightstand, thin ones, colored burgundy, navy, and mustard. The little kitchen, which she brought us to next, had a scarred round table in the corner, a few dishes behind cabinet doors made of glass. An embroidered dishcloth hung on the stove handle: flowers in a basket. "You like those, don't you?" my mother asked me when she saw me looking at it, smiling in a way that I thought conveyed misplaced pride.

"What, the flowers?"

"Yes, embroidery."

I shrugged. I only used to. She was not keeping up with us.

The living room, with its three large windows abutting each other and looking out onto the street, was the only room that had any natural light; still, my mother had the single floor lamp turned on. The only furniture was a large green sofa, its cushions nearly U-shaped, which was pushed against the windows. A well-worn burgundy rug on the floor emitted a faint smell of mothballs.

"I'll be getting some more things, of course," my mother said. "This is just for now."

Neither Sharla nor I said anything. What could she possibly get that would work against the sadness of this place—the plaster-patched walls, the creaking floorboards, the chipping tile in the bathroom, the rust stains in both sinks?

"Did you *buy* this furniture?" I asked.

"Yes," she said, with some measure of pride. "I've sold two paintings already—out in Santa Fe. People pay for my art!"

She smiled at me, then at Sharla, then at me again. Next door, someone hawked; then the toilet flushed.

"Uh-huh," I said, finally. I wanted to punch Sharla.

She wasn't saying anything. I felt as though I might as well be here alone.

As if reading my mind, my mother said, "Sharla?"

She did not respond, at first. But then, "How can you live here?" she asked.

Not my question, exactly. *Why* are you living here, is what I wanted to know. And then there was this: *Who* are you?

"It's what I can afford right now," my mother said. "Later, I hope to have my own house."

"Like Jasmine?" I asked.

"Well . . ." She went to the refrigerator, began taking things out: a package of chicken legs, lettuce. "Jasmine sold her house. Just last week."

"She did?" I had not seen any activity in Jasmine's house since she and my mother had left: no people, no sign saying the place was for sale.

"Yes. It was really quick—some family where the father got transferred. They only looked at it once, isn't that something? They'll be moving in in a few weeks."

"We're getting new neighbors?" I asked.

"Yes. I understand the children are quite young; maybe you can baby-sit."

"But . . ." It irritated me that so much could have happened unbeknownst to me. "*When* did they look at it?"

"I suppose you might have been in school."

"But what about all Jasmine's *stuff*?"

"Well, that's . . . I meant to talk to you about that. She will be having a truck come, a moving truck, next Friday. And they'll . . . Well, I'm going to use it, too. To bring my things here. Just *my* things, you know, my clothes, and so on."

"But you—"

"Jasmine will be moving back to Clear Falls, too," my mother said. "That's how we can share the truck. Isn't that lucky?"

"Where is she moving?" Sharla, now. Angry.

"Nearby, I think," my mother said.

She turned slowly, faced us. "You know, she's become an awfully good friend to me. I—"

"I want to go home," Sharla said.

"Just a minute," my mother said. "Just a minute! You just *got* here! We need to *talk* about some things!"

Sharla would not look at our mother. She stood stiffly, her mouth a grim, straight line.

"Look," our mother said, her voice softer, reasoning. "You won't talk to me on the phone, not really. You won't write to me. And now you just got here and you want to leave."

Silence. The tap dripped.

Sharla continued to stare straight ahead. I thought of statues I'd seen, blankness where eyes should have been.

My mother walked partway over to Sharla, then stopped. "Sharla, I'm your *mother*, my God, I . . . *look* at me, why won't you let me *tell* you anything!"

"I'm waiting outside for Dad." Now Sharla's face was flushed; I could see she was trying not to cry. She moved toward the door.

"Sharla," my mother said quietly. "Please."

Sharla opened the door and my mother rushed to her, put her arms around her. "Will you *stop* this, will you just—"

But Sharla pulled free, and was gone, running down the dim hall.

My mother turned to me, her eyes wide and bright. "I bought chicken," she said, walking quickly back to the kitchen. "I thought I'd fry it. Mashed potatoes. And I made a cake, too, and guess what kind of frosting it has? Caramel! It's in the refrigerator, take a look." She put on an apron.

"I don't want anything," I said. "Thank you. I have to go with Sharla."

"No you don't," my mother said, her back to me. She pulled down a small sack of flour from the cupboard, began shaking it into a bowl I had never seen before. "You can stay."

"I don't want to. I really don't." I backed up slowly until I got to the door; then I, too, began running.

My father received several more phone calls in the next week from a woman whose name we learned was Georgia Anderson. And then she came for dinner.

She was a secretary at my father's office; she worked, in fact, for his boss. She was blond, blue-eyed, slightly overweight, but very pretty. She had a shy way about her, but she opened up when Sharla brought her to our bedroom. She told us she loved our room, examined with care (but without touching) our figurines, the pictures we had on our walls, the books on our nightstand, our stuffed animals. She told us she had shared a room with her sister when she was growing up, that she had loved and hated it, that they had used a piece of red yarn to divide the room exactly, that they spoke to each other at night on tin can telephones, that they got to have their own miniature Christmas tree on their dresser every year. She had brought dessert: a cherry pie she had made that was still warm from the oven, the top decorated with beautiful pastry leaves. By the time we ate it, it seemed everyone felt relaxed and happy. I loved having our table balanced again, loved seeing my father converse with someone other than Sharla and me. When my father poured coffee for the two of them, Sharla and I excused ourselves to go and do homework.

"So what do you think of her?" Sharla asked. She was lying on her stomach, her head bent over her book, her hair hiding her face.

"I don't know." I liked her.

"I like her," Sharla said.

"Me, too."

Sharla turned onto her back, stretched out luxuriously. I shut my book, did the same.

"She made the dress she was wearing," Sharla said.

"She did?" It was a beautiful green wool dress, full-skirted, with a soft bow at the neck. There was a matching green belt.

"Even the belt?"

"Yup. She sews everything: curtains, coats, table-cloths; she made Halloween costumes for all her nieces and nephews."

"How do you know?"

"She told me, when you were in the bathroom."

"I wish she'd make me something." My wardrobe was in terrible shape; we never had gotten clothes for school, and I had in fact outgrown many things. I knew a girl at school whose mother sewed for her; she always wore matching headbands with her outfits.

"Ask her." Sharla yawned. "She'll do it."

"You think?"

"I know."

"How do you know?"

"Because she really loves to sew. And she really loves Dad."

I looked quickly at Sharla, thinking of something to say that would undermine her remark, that would take away some of the strength and surety of it. But there was nothing to say. It was true.

Sharla stared back at me. She was not unhappy about this, I saw. Nor, I realized, was I. Somewhere inside, I'd been waiting for it. Now it was here. And it was not a bad thing. This weekend, we had decided, we were all going to look at Christmas displays in the store windows, then have dinner out at the fanciest restaurant we could think of.

I pushed my school books out of the way, reached for the *Seventeen* magazine Georgia had brought us as a happy-to-meet-you present. I began looking at the clothes. I wanted suggestions for all the things I could ask for now.

Georgia taught Sharla and me to sew. Sharla never kept it up after high school, but I did. I love it. There's something about the self-reliance of it all, of understanding secrets about how things are made, of being able to make invisible repairs.

Even after we could make our own clothes, Georgia still made the harder things: coats, prom dresses. And now she makes wonderful things for our children. Lately, it's quilts. My kids always open her presents first at Christmastime, and they always love what they get. They call her Grandma. I want them to. They know she's not my real mother, but they don't care. She does everything right. When my father died last year, it was Georgia who brought all of us peace. As she always had. In direct opposition to you-know-who.

*T*he week after our mother moved back, we met her at a restaurant downtown, at her request. It was a small Italian place, dimly lit, red-and-white-checked table-cloths. Our father dropped us off, and we found our mother at a corner table. She stood, embraced us briefly, then sat down, her face grim.

"What's wrong with you?" Sharla asked.

"Nothing. What do you mean?"

"You look mad."

"I'm not mad."

Silence.

She picked up the menu, her voice high and pleasant. "So! What kind of pizza would you like?"

"I want spaghetti and meatballs," Sharla said.

"Well, I'm sorry, but you'll have to agree on a pizza. I can't afford three entrées. I thought we could just share a pizza."

Sharla put down the menu. "I don't care then, you pick. I don't really like pizza."

My mother looked up, surprised. "Since when?"

Sharla shrugged, turned her head away, studied the wall.

My mother leaned back in her chair, sighed. Then she sat up and moved in close to Sharla, spoke quietly. "You know, I have had just about enough from you."

"*What?*" Sharla said. "What did I do?"

"Your saying you don't like pizza, for starters, that's just deliberately—"

"I DON'T like pizza!" Sharla yelled. The few other patrons turned to look at us, then away.

"Don't you raise your voice," my mother said. "You show some respect for the other people trying to have a nice dinner here, if you can't show respect to me."

"She really doesn't like pizza anymore," I said. "She said that last week."

"Shut up," Sharla told me.

I sat back in my chair, hurt. Then, "*You* shut up," I said.

My mother put her coat on, picked up her purse. "Suppose we just not do this," she said. "Suppose you two just go home. I know you'd rather be there, anyway. I don't have to do this. I do *not* have to do this. I have feelings, too. I have limits."

I looked at Sharla, incredulous at my mother's behavior. Sharla was smiling, the smirk variety. But I saw that she was afraid.

My mother called my father from the restaurant's pay phone. He had just gotten home, but he came right back. When we got into the car, I saw him staring out the window at my mother with an expression full of only pity. He drove off in such a way as to make me think he was trying to be gentle. My mother got smaller in the distance, then disappeared.

"I told you she was crazy," Sharla said, when we were in bed that night, the lights out.

"I think she just got mad."

"Why? Who would yell at their kids because they don't like pizza anymore?"

"She didn't yell."

"Same thing," Sharla said.

I turned my pillow over, shut my eyes. Lately, when I went to sleep, I made a fist and laid it over my heart. I did this now, then bent down to suck at my knuckle.

"What are you *do*ing over there?" Sharla asked.

"Nothing."

"Well, do it quieter."

On Christmas Eve, our father pulled up in front of our mother's house. I got out of the car and waited for Sharla, who did not budge. "Hurry up!" I said. "It's cold!"

She did not move.

"Sharla?" my father said.

She closed her eyes, leaned her head back against the seat.

"Come on!" I said, and then watched, amazed, as she lay down on the seat and began sobbing.

My father sat dumbstruck for a moment, then called to me to get back in the car. I climbed into the backseat, slammed the door behind me.

I had never heard Sharla cry this way. It sounded like fake laughter. My father pulled the car closer to the curb, turned off the engine, put his hand on Sharla's back.

"Sharla? What is it?"

"I can't," she said, her voice muffled and sounding as though she had a cold. "Please don't make me go in there. I just can't."

"Sharla, it's Christmas Eve," my father said. "She's your mother."

She sat up, wiped furiously at her face. "You're getting divorced!"

"Yes, we are," my father said carefully. "But she is still your mother. She will always be your mother."

"I don't WANT her to be!" Sharla yelled. "I don't want her anymore! Dad, you don't know what it's like to go and see her. She's crazy now!"

"She's not crazy," he said. "She's different, that's true. But she's not crazy. And Sharla, you know she loves you very much."

"I can't go in there."

We sat. The car began to get cold, and my father started the engine, turned the heater up full blast. I looked up to my mother's windows and saw the outline of her standing there. I slumped down further in the backseat, looked away.

Finally, my father said, "I'll tell you what, Sharla. Just go and visit for a few hours; you don't have to spend the night, all right?"

She did not answer.

"Can you just do that, honey?"

"No!" she said, her voice breaking, and she sat up and held on to the lapels of my father's coat, sobbing loudly again, begging him to take her home.

He stroked her head, looked over into the backseat at me.

I shook my head.

"You don't want to go back home?" he asked quietly.

"No," I said. "I don't want to go to Mom's either."

"All right," he sighed. "All right. Just let me go up and tell her. Let me talk to her."

I watched my father walk up the steps to the building and go in. I saw my mother leave the window to let him in.

"I just can't visit her anymore," Sharla said.

"I know."

"But you can, Ginny."

"I don't want to, either."

I knew what Sharla was feeling: the pull to a mother versus the great discomfort of spending time with a stranger who asked too much of you. Sharla said our mother was beginning to act desperate, that when she thought of her, she saw a creature with large, watery eyes, trembling lips, and claws for hands. I knew what she meant, though my image of my mother was tempered by some measure of compassion: I could see how much she hurt. But I could not give her what she wanted. Not the things she named, such as living with her at least part-time; not the things she did not name that were the things she wanted most, such as a move back inside me to the lit place she used to occupy. That place was gone.

In a few minutes, our father came back out of the building and got into the car. His face was a mix of sorrow and mild determination. "I wonder if you could just—"

Sharla put her hand on his arm. "Could we please go home, Dad? You said we could go home."

He waited a long moment, then drove slowly away from the curb. I looked back up at the window. She was not there.

"She could come to the house and see you, how about that?" my father asked.

"No," Sharla said quickly.

I agreed with her. The house was our safe place, our father's place. She had come back only once, to supervise the two moving men who loaded her things onto the truck with Jasmine's. She had pointed to her closet, to the china cabinet holding the incomplete set of dishes she'd gotten from her mother, to her sewing basket and knitting supplies, to a Queen Anne chair that had belonged to her grandmother. She did not take much, really. But it seemed to me that the house echoed for some time after she left, then fell deeply silent until just recently, when sounds of a normal life had begun there again.

When we got home, our father gave us each the presents our mother had given him to give to us. The packages were identically shaped, large and flat; paintings, I'd guessed. I had no desire to open mine; nor, I suspected, did Sharla. We put them under the tree with the presents we had waiting there, from our father and Georgia—Georgia had already given us Advent calendars, which we had hung over our beds. Then our father made us cocoa with marshmallows and sat us at the kitchen table.

"I want you to tell me what's so hard for you when you see your mother," he said. "Maybe we can work some things out."

"Did she feel bad?" I asked. It came out too bright and eager; I hadn't meant to sound that way.

"She . . . yes, it hurt her a lot that you wouldn't come in. She's trying, you know."

"She's trying too hard," Sharla said. "It makes you feel weird."

"She's having kind of a bad time right now," our father said.

"She left," Sharla said. "For no reason."

No one said anything else for a long time. And then my father said, "I believe she thinks she has reasons."

226

"Dad," Sharla said. "Please, can we just not see her for a while? I need some time away from her."

We hadn't seen her very often, only a few visits to her house and the time at the restaurant. But I knew what Sharla meant. Whenever we saw our mother, something always happened that made us uncomfortable. One night, Jasmine had shown up, seeming to surprise my mother. "Oh!" she'd said, after she opened the door. "Jasmine! But . . . well, the girls are here."

"Oh, God," Jasmine said. Then their voices got too low for us to hear. And then Jasmine came into the little kitchen.

I'd forgotten how darkly beautiful she was, how exotic looking.

"How *are* you?" she'd asked us, kissing our cheeks. Her perfume was spicy, overpowering.

"Fine," Sharla said, staring down at her plate.

"I wish you'd come and visit *me* sometime," Jasmine said.

"Where do you live?" I asked.

"I've got to give you the address," she said. But she left a few minutes later without doing so.

"We get together quite a bit," my mother said, sitting down at the table after Jasmine had left. "We do things, you know, movies . . ."

"Dad got a raise," Sharla said.

"Did he?"

"Yup." She loaded up a fork with macaroni and cheese, talked through it. "A big one." She put more in her mouth, then said, "Ishn't that good?"

I watched my mother watching her. "Sharla," she said

finally, and I knew what she meant: Don't talk with your mouth full.

"*What?*" Sharla said.

My mother looked away, said nothing more. I felt sorry for her for a moment; then the softness in my stomach turned to a hard knot of contempt.

When I was out jogging last week, I saw a woman walking a dog. Only it was the classic case of the dog walking *her*. The woman was laughing a bit, taking giant strides in an effort to keep up, but she was clearly embarrassed. The dog strained at the leash; the woman's arm looked practically pulled out of the socket. I wanted to go over there and jerk that leash out of the woman's hands, smack the dog's butt with it. "Don't let him do that!" I wanted to say. "Why are you letting him *do* that?"

I was a bit surprised by my strong reaction: for one thing, it was none of my business. But I think my response was tied up with things like what I just remembered, that feeling of contempt you have for someone you see is not in control when you want them to be.

It's funny how, oftentimes, the people you love the most are given the least margin for error. Funny, too, the places where the anger ends up surfacing.

Later on that Christmas Eve when Sharla and I left without seeing her, our mother called us. She asked that Sharla and I each get on an extension. Then she asked if we had opened our presents.

"No," Sharla said, and I followed quickly with, "We're waiting for tomorrow."

"I kind of wanted to be there when you opened them," my mother said.

Neither Sharla nor I said anything. Georgia was coming on Christmas Day. We had plans.

"I'm sorry you didn't feel you were able to come up," she continued. "I'm not blaming you—it's been awkward. You know, we're all just going to have to go through this time of transition. It's hard. I'm sure all of us have said or done things we wish we hadn't. But we'll get through this. I want you both to know I love you very much. Nothing you can do will ever change that. We'll get through this."

Silence. I remember thinking, *we're* through it. You're the only one who's having trouble.

"Could you maybe open your presents now, so I could at least hear you doing it?"

"I'll get them," I said quickly, before Sharla could refuse. I brought Sharla's gift to her in the living room, took mine back to the kitchen.

"We can open them together," I said, and started unwrapping my gift, then stopped, listening to see if I could hear Sharla doing the same. She was; I could hear the rustling sounds.

"Thanks, Mom," Sharla said quietly. "It's pretty."

I finished opening my gift. It was a painting of a mother sitting in a rocker holding a baby. The room was furnished ordinarily: a crib, a night table with a softly glowing lamp, a yellow, fringed rug. But where the walls should have been were thin, white clouds against a black night sky, pinpoints of stars were everywhere.

"Thank you," I said.

"Do you like it?"

My throat ached. I nodded, then croaked, "Yes." I was so sorry we hadn't gone up to her apartment. It was Christmas Eve; she was all alone. Nor had we gotten her a present—every time our father offered to take us to get her something, we'd told him we were going to do it ourselves.

"I'll bring you your present tomorrow night," I said. Something would be open. Or I'd make something.

"I'll bring mine, too," Sharla said. I heard some reluctant sorrow in her voice as well.

Our mother said nothing for a while, breathed into the phone. Then, "Well, you know, I won't be home tomorrow night. Remember how you were going to have breakfast with me and then go right home? So I . . . well, I have train tickets for a trip to New York City early tomorrow afternoon. I'm going to stay in a hotel and see all the sights! I'll bring you back something. What would you like?"

"Who are you going with?" Sharla asked.

But we knew. And in that instant—and I felt it happen to both of us at the same time, as though Sharla and I shared a heart and a brain and a soul—at that instant, we let go of something.

"Jasmine and I are going together," my mother said. "But if you girls would like to have breakfast with me—"

"Have fun," Sharla said, and hung up.

"Merry Christmas," I said, and it seemed so odd to be saying that over the phone, to my mother.

"Ginny?" she said, and I hung up.

I went into the living room, saw Sharla sitting with a canvas in her lap. Her painting was of a bird wearing high heels, pearls, and an apron, sitting chained to a tree with tiny pot holders for leaves. The sun in the sky was blue.

"Where's Dad?" I asked. I wondered if he'd heard any of the conversation.

"In the basement. He's finishing building something. I think it's a bookcase for us, a fancy one."

"Did you peek?"

She smiled.

"What's it like?" I asked.

"It's beautiful."

I looked at the painting in her lap. "That's nice, too," I tried; but my voice betrayed me.

"It doesn't make any sense," Sharla said. And then, looking up at me, "Jasmine and Mom are girlfriends, you know."

"I know."

"No. I mean, lesbos. Lesbians."

I stepped back.

"They are," Sharla said.

"No, they are not."

She snorted. "I knew I couldn't tell you."

My mind felt crowded with images that wanted in. Somewhere inside, I pulled a curtain. Not yet. Not yet.

I put the painting behind my dresser; Sharla put hers in her closet. We celebrated Christmas with my father and Georgia, who, at the end of January, became his fiancée.

In February, my mother moved back to Santa Fe. We did not see her on the day she left, nor in the weeks before. Our visits to her had fizzled and died. No one fought hard enough to keep them alive. Sharla had told our father about her suspicions regarding Jasmine and our mother. "What did he *say*?" I asked, and Sharla said, "Nothing. He must have known."

We got letters, but not with the frequency we had at first. And once when she called, when I came into the kitchen to have my time alone with her, I simply let the phone rest on the counter. I stared at it while I made a braid in my hair, then unbraided it. I picked some dirt from beneath my fingernails, counted slowly to twenty-five. Then I hung the phone up. She did not call back.

Time passed. Time passed. My father was happy. Georgia was easy, sunny. I grew to love her in a way that was not compensatory. It amazed me, how easily that happened.

Sharla and I did not write to our mother; we did not call, despite gentle urging from both our father and Georgia. First, we would not; then, it seemed, we could not.

Eventually, we got only postcards from our mother giving us her new addresses. Sometimes we saved them. Sometimes we did not. She eventually settled in California.

And then, so many years after that time of enormous change and loss, so many years later, Sharla called me to say, "Well, *I* got some news today." And before the week was out, I was on a plane to see her and a mother I'd not laid eyes on for thirty-five years.

And here I am.

*T*he walk to baggage claim seems to take forever. I see the two children I enjoyed listening to on the plane with their father way ahead of me, Martha a bit behind me. I slow down, wait for her.

"So. How was *your* ride?" I ask.

"Well, except for the part when I thought we were all going to die . . ."

"Yeah." I smile.

"You know, I wanted to tell you," Martha begins. But then she says, "Oh, never mind. Just . . . good luck."

"What? What were you going to say?"

"Well, I was just going to say that it seems one of the things you have to do in order to finally grow up is to let that what-my-parents-did-to-me stuff *go*."

I say nothing, watch my feet walking.

"But it's none of my business. Why don't I just go back to wishing you luck."

"Thanks."

Martha slows her pace a bit. I quicken mine.

When I arrive at the baggage claim, I see Sharla right away, dressed in jeans and a black sweater, a black suede jacket over her shoulders. She is wearing a belt with a huge silver buckle and fabulous-looking cowboy boots. She always looks as if she walked off of the pages of a magazine; I always look as though I am on the way to a meeting with the minister. It's funny; I always thought Sharla would be the conservative one. But as we grew up, Sharla became the risk-taker, the wilder one.

Now I scan her face, trying not to look anxious, but failing. "Oh, for God's sake, I'm all *right*," she says.

I embrace her hard, say into her ear, "Oh, Sharla, I'm so sorry."

She pulls away from me. "Hey. It's not for sure, remember? I'll know on Friday."

"How can they do that? How can they say, 'You might be terminally ill. We'll let you know in a few days.' How can they *do* that?"

"Well, it's complicated," Sharla says.

"What do you mean?"

"Why don't you get your bags. We'll talk on the way."

I remember, all of a sudden, where we are, that we are here to see our mother. "Why am I not surprised that she didn't bother to pick us up?"

"I told her not to," Sharla said. "I wanted some time with you first. To get ready."

"Yeah, well, maybe that was a good idea." I see my small bag coming out, drag it off the belt.

"That's all you brought?" Sharla asks.

"We're only staying three days, right?"

"Yeah, but . . ." She shrugs. "I've got more." She points to a pile of floral French luggage; there are four pieces.

"What did you *bring*?" I ask.

"I was nervous."

"So, what, you've got bags full of tranquilizers?"

"No, just one vial."

"Really?"

"Just Valium."

"Can I have some?"

She pulls a slim plastic bottle from her purse. "One?"

"How many milligrams?"

"Five."

"I'll take two."

"That's a lot."

"Okay, one. Oh, never mind. Forget it."

Sharla puts the vial back in her purse. Then she loads her bags onto a cart. "I've got a car waiting." She pulls her sunglasses out of her pocket, puts them on. If she's ill, she sure doesn't look it.

"Did you get a stretch limo?" I ask hopefully. "White?"

"You're so tacky."

"Well. That, or honest."

"Saying you want a white stretch is not honest, it's tacky," Sharla says. "Trust me." She sighs. "Where'd you get that *blouse*?"

The drive into Marin County is beautiful. Outside our windows is the breathtaking combination of sea and sky and land that you see in movies and think, Oh sure, show me where *that* is. But here it is.

"I can't believe I'm so old and have never been here before," I say.

Sharla looks at me over the top of her sunglasses.

"I know, but you could come here and not see *her*. I'm not sure I'd recognize her if I *did* see her."

"I think you'd recognize her," Sharla says, looking again out her window. Then, "God," she says softly, in appreciation of the spectacular view of houses nestled into the hilltops. "How much does one of those houses on top of the hill go for?" she asks the driver.

"Millions," he says.

"Yes," Sharla says, "but how many millions?"

" 'Spose I said only one million. Could you afford it then?"

"No."

"So what's the difference?"

Sharla and I look at each other, squelch a giggle. Contrary to what we've been told, not everybody in California is in a good mood all the time.

"Just curious," Sharla says.

"Well, it's more than one million, I'll tell you that."

"I see. Well. Thank you *very* much." She settles back against the seat, looks over at me. "Thanks for coming, Ginny." She is speaking very quietly, so Mr. Congeniality can't hear us.

"Well, of course I came."

"It's maybe just a cyst."

"It's on your ovary?"

"Yeah. But maybe it's just a cyst."

I take in a breath, steady myself. "When do they—"

"You know what?" Sharla says. "For days, I've been talking about nothing but this with Jonathan. I'm sort of sick of it. I mean, if it is, it is, I'll deal with it. I'd really like this time to be . . . free of that."

"You want to just lighten up a bit," I say. "Forget about things."

"Yeah."

"Just . . . oh, you know, come and see your mother, who walked out of your life over thirty years ago, whom you've not seen since. A kind of spa, you might say."

Sharla smiles. "You know, I don't know if she really did that or not. I've been thinking a lot about it, and I don't know if you could say she really walked out."

"She *left* us."

Sharla begins to answer me, but then, as we start going up a steep hill on a heavily wooded road, she asks, "Is this Summit already?"

"That's what the sign says," the driver mutters.

"Hey!" I say, loudly, and Sharla nudges me with her boot.

"No," I tell her. And then, to the driver, "*Hey!*"

He looks at me in the rearview. "Yes?"

"Could you just . . . aren't you supposed to be polite?"

"Yeah. I'm not being polite enough?"

I sigh, let it go. There are more important things to think about.

"God. We're there," Sharla says.

"But we didn't *talk* about anything," I say. "I don't think I'm ready!"

"Well, the scenery. I just wanted to see it. I thought it would take longer to get here." The car pulls into a driveway. Number 330 is stenciled on the garage. The house is evidently out of sight, down the hill, as were many of the houses we passed. The driver puts the car into park, starts filling out some paperwork. I feel my hands tighten on my purse, take a huge breath.

"Should we ask him to drive around for a while?" Sharla whispers. I look at the back of his head, the dejected slump of his shoulders.

"No," I say. And then it comes to me to give him a tip, just to see his face. Sharla signs for the bill, and I pull a twenty out of my purse, hand it over the seat.

"What's this?" he asks.

"A tip."

"Included," he says.

"Extra," I insist.

His face softens, reluctantly. Then, "Sorry," he says. "I'm not feeling well today. I'm sorry. 'Shouldn't have come to work. But I need the money." He laughs. "I'll carry your bags in twice, okay?"

"No, thanks," we say together. And I know why. The moment is crowded enough already.

It takes us two trips to bring the luggage down to the door of a beautiful, brown-shingled house with leaded glass windows. Flowers are everywhere—in window boxes, in scattered gardens. The landscape around the house is softly controlled, but still has a feeling of wildness. We can see the living room through one window; there is a piano there, some large, soft pieces of furniture, deep green; a Persian rug, many vases of flowers, a grandmother clock, paintings everywhere. I knock, we wait a breathless moment, and the door opens. And there she is. And Sharla is right, I would know her anywhere.

I start to say something, then put my hands over my face. I feel her pulling both of us toward her, saying syllables that are not words, that could not be, not if they were going to contain all that she is saying. A memory comes to me of my younger daughter, whom I overheard playacting with a friend the other day. "I am *dy*ing of a *mul*titude of *feel*ings," she was saying, in what she calls her "opera voice." She was wearing a number of scarves as veils, and her friend, who was supposed to pull them off one at a time, yanked at the top one, only to have them all fall down.

* * *

"I didn't think I was going to cry like that," Sharla says. We are lying in the guest room, taking a break before dinner, which our mother has insisted on preparing alone. Probably she wants to give us all some time to recover. "Did you?"

"I thought I might," I say. "I thought either that, or I'd start laughing."

Sharla looks at me, puzzled.

"You know," I say. "Like when you shouldn't. Like at a funeral. So you do."

Sharla lies down on the bed, pulls her sweater up to expose her belly, pats it. "I'm hungry, are you?"

"Yeah. It smells good, whatever it is."

"Something Italian, I think, lots of garlic."

"Let's go taste," I say.

"In a minute."

"She's still beautiful, don't you think?"

"Yeah. I love her hair."

It was completely gray now, but beautifully streaked. It was long; she wore it up in a bun. She was tan, a little too thin, perhaps. She wore dangling silver earrings with a green, arty T-shirt and loose, black tie pants. Her make-up was subtle: eyeliner, a bit of rust-colored lipstick.

"She still seems so familiar, even though she's so different," I say. "I shouldn't be surprised. But I am anyway. I guess I just didn't know what to expect."

"If you'd just . . . met her," Sharla says, "like at a party or something, wouldn't you like her? I mean, doesn't she seem like a pretty neat woman?"

"Yeah. She turned out just fine."

Sharla laughs. "It feels like we're talking about our children."

"Well, there always *was* that, you know? I think we always felt like we kind of had to take care of her."

"I guess," Sharla says.

I get up, walk over to the window. "It's so beautiful here. Look at the view she has every day. She's really done well for herself."

Sharla comes over to stand beside me, puts her arm around me. "Ginny."

"What?" I put my arm around her. This is the part where she is going to tell me she already knows the outcome of the biopsy, and that it's not good.

"I have to tell you something."

Here it is. "Yes?"

"That cyst thing? It's not what I told you."

I'll put her in my living room so she'll be close to everything. I'll get someone to stay with her whenever I have to leave.

Sharla sits on the wide windowsill, looks up at me. "It's not me who's sick. It's her."

It takes a moment for my thoughts to reshuffle. Then, "What?" I say.

"It's her. It's her who's sick. Mom."

"How do you know?"

"She called me."

I start to laugh, stop. "So . . . why didn't you tell me?"

She sighs. "I was afraid you wouldn't come."

"Huh," I say. It is the only word that can escape from the tangled goings-on in my mind.

"Would you have?"

I see the scene: the phone rings. I pick it up. Sharla says

our mother is sick. Naturally I think she means Georgia. But then she says no, it's our birth mother. You know, *Mom.* And if I am honest, I must admit that the first thought that would come to me would be, That's her problem. Followed by, What am *I* supposed to do about it?

When our father died, where was my mother? Nowhere in sight, that's where. We wrote her about it, and heard nothing back. Of course, we did request that she not come to the funeral. We felt it would be too upsetting, on top of everything else.

But if Sharla had told me about our mother, surely, after an initial reaction of numbness, I would have rallied to do the right thing. Which would be to come here.

I start for the door.

"Don't," Sharla says. "She wanted to make us dinner first. I wasn't supposed to tell you until after. But I couldn't wait anymore."

"I'm going out there."

"Don't tell her I told you. Please."

I look at her face: pleading, even a bit frightened.

"I won't tell her," I say. "I'll just offer to help. I'll say I was getting bored."

"All right," Sharla says. "I'm going to pee. I'll be down in a minute."

From the hall, I hear the pleasant banging of pots and pans. I enter the kitchen to see my mother standing at the sink with her back to me. She is humming softly to herself; she doesn't know I'm here. But then she turns around quickly, gasps.

"Sorry," I say. "I didn't mean to scare you."

"No, it's just . . . Well, I wanted to have dinner all

ready, so we could sit down and really talk, without dis-
tractions. And I guess . . . I don't know, I guess I'm a little
nervous."

"Why don't you let me help you?" I ask. "I want to
play with your fancy stuff." My mother has a kitchen
right out of a decorating magazine: smaller, perhaps, but
as well-equipped and as beautiful: professional-looking
pans hanging from a cook's rack, a subzero refrigerator,
granite counters, a Garland stove, little sinks within
sinks.

She smiles, hands me a grater and a few peeled carrots.

"For the sauce," she says. "I'm making eggplant
parmigiana; I put carrots in to sweeten it a bit. Also a
little honey. Do you ever do that, Ginny?"

And now something happens for which I have no ex-
planation whatsoever: I feel my legs weaken, buckle beneath me, and suddenly I am sitting on the floor.

My mother rushes over to me, and then Sharla, too,
who has just come into the kitchen. "What happened?"
my mother says. "What happened here?"

"I'm fine," I say, and start to get up. But then I feel a
bit dizzy, so I sit back down. Well, I got almost no sleep
last night; that's all it is. The scotch I had on the plane,
that's what it is.

My mother takes the grater out of my hand. "Did you
slip? Is the floor wet?"

Sharla sits down beside me. "Are you okay?"

"I'm fine!" I say. "I don't know what happened! I was
just all of a sudden on the floor!" I look around myself.
"Which is not such a bad place to be. It's nice down here.
I like your tiles, Mom."

My mother sits down on the floor with us. "Mexican," she says. "I like them much better than the Italian."

"Your whole house is so beautiful," I say.

"Thank you."

"You must make a fortune."

She smiles. "I do all right. Just in the last couple years, though." She reaches up on the counter for the carrots I was going to grate, gives us each one. "Eat this," she tells me. "Maybe you're too hungry."

"Did you do all the paintings in here?" I ask.

My mother takes a bite of her carrot. "All but three," she says. "Some friends did the one in your room and two of the ones in the dining room."

"Huh," I say. And then, "Mom, are you sick?"

My mother looks quickly at Sharla, who looks murderously at me. Then Sharla says quietly, "I'm sorry. I had to tell her."

"Well," my mother says. "Apparently so. But I've got a while before the train leaves the station. And I'm so glad you're here." She takes a deep breath, smiles. "Gosh. I don't know how in the world we'll say all we need to."

A long moment. Finally, I stand, reach for an open bottle of wine, bring it down to our impromptu social circle. I sniff it. "Is this any good?"

My mother nods. "I'll get some glasses."

"Don't bother." I take a swig from the bottle, then pass it to her.

She laughs, stares at me with a deep and clear affection. And then she takes a drink and passes the bottle to Sharla.

I lean back against the cupboard. "We could just stay here for the evening," I say.

No one says anything for a long while. Birds twitter occasionally outside the kitchen windows. Otherwise, there is silence. We pass the bottle around the circle a few times, eat our carrots. Then Sharla says, "Well, I don't know about you. But my ass is too old for this action." She stands up. "Come on. Let's go get comfortable."

I'll just finish dinner," my mother says.

I turn off the flame under the saucepan. "Mom."

She laughs. "Okay." She removes her apron, picks up the phone, and dials a number. "Henry? It's Marion. I need a big order as soon as you can get it here." Then, to us, "Do you both still like Chinese?"

All around the TV room are tiny white boxes and empty wine bottles. Sharla has put her chopsticks in her hair to hold it off her neck; the effect is lovely. We are each lying on our own little sofa; the room has three of them, all out of floral chintz, arranged in a U-shape. In the background, the jazz station is playing softly.

"I had to stay away from playgrounds for a long time," my mother says. "I passed by one soon after I first left, and I just fell apart. Same thing with schools. Dime stores. And oh, the girls' section of any department store!"

Neither Sharla nor I speak. My eyes are closed. I'm a little bit dizzy again.

"I used to . . . Well, this may sound odd. But what really brought me comfort was going to big university bookstores and looking at the physics books."

My eyes snap open at this. I can't believe we both seek

solace in science, and that we never new this about each other. You can't get away from some things. You say you're turning your back on someone, and you start off down a long road, and you walk so very far, and then you find out the road is just a big circle and you are back where you started. I laugh to myself, close my eyes again.

"I didn't really understand them," my mother says, "but the illustrations were so graceful, and the writing seemed so wise and compassionate. Those books told me there was a logic to everything—maybe it was beyond my comprehension, but there was a logic, a reason for things happening. It made me see that humans are very small and insignificant; that all our triumphs and errors don't really amount to much at all. There are times that notion can scare you, or depress you; but there are other times when thinking about it can help you sleep. Things like—well, I would read something like the first law of thermodynamics, and just find it enormously comforting. I still do. Think of it, the notion of nothing ever being lost, of it just changing form."

"Is that the first law?" Sharla asks.

"That's what it suggests."

"What's the second law?" I ask.

"Beats me," my mother says. And then, "*Is* there a second?"

For some reason—the level of alcohol in our blood, perhaps—we find this all very funny, and we laugh long and loudly.

Then, "Mom?" I say. "Whatever happened to Jasmine Johnson?"

A rich silence. Then my mother says softly, "Oh, well,

Jasmine and I lived together for two years. Then she had to move again, and I didn't want to go with her."

"Was her husband some gangster or something?" I say.

"Maybe. All I knew for sure was that he was someone very rich and powerful and that he liked to smack his wife around, keep her under his thumb. Jasmine knew he would never give her a divorce. So she just ran from him."

"Her poor son," I say. "God, he was cute, that Wayne."

"You knew he was her son?" my mother asks.

"He told me."

"Huh. That was dangerous."

"I think he also knew that his mother was a lesbian," I say. "But he was very cool about it. Which was quite a thing for those times."

"What did you say?" my mother asks.

"That he knew. That Jasmine was a lesbian."

"But she wasn't."

I sit up, look at her. "Come on, Mom."

"She wasn't! I knew her very, very well; and believe me, she was not. She was different from most women, yes; she was . . . a sensualist, she believed in people doing a lot more than they allowed themselves to do ordinarily; but no, she was not a lesbian."

Sharla sits up now, too. Her eye makeup is smudged beneath one eye, her impromptu hairdo completely off kilter. "But Mom, you . . . Weren't you and Jasmine—?"

And now my mother is sitting up, too. "Were we together? In that way?" She laughs. "Oh God, no!"

"I was sure you were," Sharla says quietly. "I was *sure* you were. I told *Dad* you were!"

"Well," my mother says. "I think he was *very* well aware of the fact that Jasmine's sexual preference was for men."

"What do you mean?" I say. My chest hurts. I am finding it hard to breathe.

My mother picks up a chopstick, threads it through her fingers. "He did sleep with her," she says quietly.

I look at Sharla, who is staring wide-eyed at our mother. "Mom," she says. "This is serious. It is so important that you tell us the *truth* now."

My mother looks at Sharla with a fragile weariness. "Yes," she says. "I know. Once everything started, I always tried to. But I could never tell you about Jasmine and your father, not when you were so young. Not when I had just moved out and you were so vulnerable, so dependent on him. And then things just . . . fell apart."

I lie back down on the sofa. I think of my father, whom I loved so much. I cannot tell him anything, now. I want to dig him up and shake him.

"Oh, my God," I say, finally. And then, "So is that why you left, Mom?"

"Oh no. No. That was part of it. But him doing that just forced the issue. I mostly left because I wasn't living a true life. I had something in me that needed out so badly. There was a night your father and I had a terrible fight and I—"

"We were awake," Sharla says.

My mother looks at her. "You were?"

Sharla nods.

"Oh, I'm so sorry you heard that; what must you have felt? I was so confused. I thought after I got straightened out, I could come back for you. I thought my leaving would be like a break in the circle of you girls and me, that I'd come back and still have a place. But the circle closed, and I was on the outside, and I couldn't get back in. And then you were just . . . gone from me. And frankly, it began to seem to me that you would be better off without me. The times I saw you, I could see how uncomfortable you were with me. No matter how I tried to explain things, I only confused you, hurt you. Well, I was so confused myself—best friends with a woman who had slept with my husband!"

"You just . . . forgave her?" Sharla asks.

My mother smiles, a faraway look in her eyes. "In an odd way, I ended up being happy she'd done what she did. She forced me to do something I wanted to do, gave me an excuse for doing it. And, she . . . had a way. You couldn't resist her. You remember, don't you? Anyway, I floundered about so badly for so long, while your father was basically very stable and kind. He loved you very much; he had a fine job; he could give you a good home. He ended up marrying a nice woman, at least she seemed like a nice woman. I saw you a few times with her and you all seemed happy."

"You saw us together?" I say. "When?"

"Shortly after he married her. I would go to places you went—restaurants, movie theaters—hoping to run into you. And I would see you, sometimes. I knew you didn't want me in your life anymore. I just . . . I had to be sure you were all right."

"I don't think I can stand this whole conversation," I say. "This is ridiculous. For one thing, you . . . Mom, are you really sick? Are you?"

She comes to sit beside me, takes my hands. "I know

how strange this all feels. Yes, I am sick. I have ovarian cancer. But there's every chance that I can survive for a while with the treatments they'll give me. But just in case I don't, I wanted to try to see you two. I had to."

I look at Sharla, whose expression is curiously blank. *"So?"* I say to her, meaning, What next? *Now* what do we do?

Sharla shrugs. "So it's two in the morning—later for us. I guess we just go to bed."

In fact, that is exactly what we do.

In the morning, I wake up alone. I go out into the kitchen to see Sharla and my mother sitting at the table, looking at a tattered book together.

"Good morning," my mother says.

I nod irritably. My mouth is stuck to itself and I have a headache that makes the bright light unbearable. I pour myself a cup of coffee with hands that want very much to shake.

"Hangover?" Sharla asks brightly.

"No."

I sit at the table and Sharla slides a bottle of aspirin toward me. I take three without looking at her.

"What's that?" I ask, gesturing toward the book.

"It's something you two used to love," my mother says. "Your clown book. You used to fight over it."

"I remember that! Let me see." I flip through the book, and each illustration is so familiar to me. I can't help smiling.

"She has lots of them," Sharla says.

"Our old books?"

"Uh-huh."

"That's where they went!" Years before, I had searched the house, looking for the books I'd been read as a child. I'd wanted to read them to my own girls. But I couldn't find them.

"I'm sorry," my mother said. "I took them when I moved. I suppose I hoped I'd read them to my grandchildren someday. But then, everything got lost."

"Not lost," I say. "Only changed."

"Well." She smiles.

"I know," I say. "I told someone on the plane I hadn't seen my mother in thirty-five years and she was absolutely incredulous. And so was I, when I heard myself."

"Oh, it . . . happened," my mother says.

For a moment, the only sound is from the wind in the trees outside.

"I would have been a good grandmother, though, I think," my mother says. "I was always good with babies."

Some wall inside me breaks. "Jesus," I say, my hand to my mouth. "I'm so sorry."

"You didn't do it," my mother says. "It just happened. I'm the one who didn't stay around to fight for you. I gave up. At that time in my life, it seemed like the right decision."

"Maybe it was," Sharla said. "We're all right, we turned out all right. We're happy."

"Are you?" my mother asks, and her voice is as wistful and plaintive as a young child's.

I nod my head. "Yeah."

"Ah," my mother says. "Then." She sighs deeply, closes her eyes, opens them. "I have wanted to know that for such a long time."

She goes to the window, looks outside. "Want to take

a walk? It's beautiful here; I have a certain way that I go. Would you like to see it?"

And because we are finally, finally ready, we tell her yes.

*I*t's the same captain on this plane going home that I had coming out; I recognize his voice. And once again, he is pointing out things we should look at: in this case, Lake Michigan. But I don't bother to open the shade.

I am thinking about the way that life can be so slippery; the way that a twelve-year-old girl looking into the mirror to count freckles reaches out toward herself and her reflection has turned into that of a woman on her wedding day, righting her veil. And how, when that bride blinks, she reopens her eyes to see a frazzled young mother trying to get lipstick on straight for the parent-teacher conference that starts in three minutes. And how after that young woman bends down to retrieve the wild-haired doll her daughter has left on the bathroom floor, she rises up a forty-seven-year-old, looking in the mirror to count age spots.

Before we left our mother's house, Sharla and I presented an abbreviated version of as many life events as we could recall: our graduations and weddings, our children's milestones; and smaller things, too: my bout with mononucleosis at age sixteen, for example. "Did you wrap a warm washcloth around your neck?" my mother asked.

"No."

"Oh well, that can feel so good when your throat hurts. I would have done that for you. And made some soup."

A long silence. And then, "What kind?" I asked.

"Well," she said. "We would have had a conference. On paper. Because I wouldn't have wanted to make you talk."

I suppose I might have written 'split pea,' " I said.

"All right," my mother said. "So first I would have gotten a good ham bone."

This is what we did, Sharla and I, on our walks with our mother. We gave her our life events to reconstruct so that she could put herself there. The three of us stood at the edge of the Pacific and our mother told us how she would have told Sharla's boyfriends that she wasn't home on the days she wanted to avoid them. In the woods, we lay on soft beds of pine needles and my mother told me that children walking after age one doesn't mean a thing.

Did this help? Did it matter? Yes, and yes. In the way that it could.

For now, we are full of promises to stay in touch, to have our mother visit soon, to meet her grandchildren ("My grandchildren!" she'd said, with her hand to her throat). We'd talked about the wisdom of introducing our children, old as they are, to someone who may very well die soon, and concluded that so might any of us.

I am thinking again about Wayne, too, remembering how easily I let him into my life, then out of it. I am thinking of how right he was when he said that people want to be deceived. I have learned the truth of that notion over and over; but I never admitted to its obvious presence in my own life. After all, I claimed I did not need my mother. I said I had replaced her.

Mostly, though, I am thinking about the notion of forgiveness, wondering if I always forgave my mother or if I never did, even now. I am wondering what it is that we ask of our mothers: what do they owe us? What is it that we owe them? Before I left, I wanted to tell my mother, "Look. You were an artist, living in an oppressive atmosphere. You did what you did in order to survive. I know you never stopped loving us. I felt it."

But I did not say that; even now, I cannot say that. I expect too much from the role of mother, both as a daughter and as a mother myself. Georgia is more of my idea of how that role should be played. It is she I modeled myself after. But what do my own daughters think of me? They haven't told me. They probably don't even really know, yet. But they will. And although God knows I don't like to admit it—that in fact I never have, until now—God knows that when they tell me what they think of me as a mother, I am going to take some serious hits.

I suppose what I now believe is that we owe our mothers and our daughters the truth, and the truth is that my mother was forgiven in the way she was not forgotten. If I tried to shut her out of my mind, there were reminders of her, anyway: the odd way I crook my little finger when I write, as she does. The way I laid my hand across my babies' backs, which is the way I remember her laying her hand on me. I hear her inflections in my voice; I see her knees emerging from my bathwater. All my life, when I ate certain things, walked certain places, witnessed certain events, there she would be. Close your eyes and draw a silk scarf past your ear: that is the whisper I heard. That is the soft presence I felt.

For so many years, when I thought of my mother, I thought of her tortured looniness before she left us. I thought of her callous disregard of our obvious needs. I thought of her unspeakable differentness, and was ashamed.

But now, sitting on this airplane on my way back to the life I went on to fashion after she left, I think of her differently. I see her so many ways: sitting back on her heels at the side of the bathtub, singing softly as she washes Sharla's and my backs; watching at the window for the six o'clock arrival of our father; wrapping Christmas presents on the wide expanse of her bed; biting her lip as she stood before the open cupboards, making out the grocery list; leaning out the kitchen window that last summer to call Sharla and me in for supper. Most clearly, though, I see her sitting at the kitchen table, in her old, usual spot. There is a cup of coffee before her, but she doesn't drink it. Instead, she stares out the window. I see the sharp angle of her cheekbone, the beautiful whitish down at the side of her face, illuminated by the sun. Her hands are quiet, resting in the cloth bowl of her apron. She sits still as a statue—waiting, I see now; she was always waiting.

The captain is going on about the sunset now, and I lift the shade impatiently, as if that will shut him up. But he is right in asking us to look; the sun is a rare, deep red, sinking slowly into bruised-looking clouds colored purple and black. I watch carefully, not seeing any movement yet. I will soon, though. You think the sun will hang in the sky forever, but once it reaches a certain point in its descent, it goes so fast—flattens, seems to hover for one instant, and is gone. Then comes the darkness, which we illuminate artificially while we wait for the new day, for the rising up again of what once seemed lost.

Joy School
by Elizabeth Berg

Katie, who is only 13, has moved to her new Missouri town, living alone with a stern, inaccessible father following her mother's death. Unable to fit in at school, she forges alliances where she can: with her housekeeper, with a fellow misfit named Cynthia, and with the beautiful Taylor, who gets her thrills out of shoplifting. Yet the most frustrating of Katie's friendships is her schoolgirl crush on the handsome 23-year-old gas station owner who shares her love of checkers but doesn't return her crush. What's a girl to do?

Published by Ballantine Books.
Available at bookstores everywhere.

Until the Real Thing Comes Along

by Elizabeth Berg

What's a single, professional thirty-something woman to do when her biological clock is ticking and there are no prospects? Patty Anne Murphy has the solution. She will beg, plead and somehow convince her gay best friend to play daddy. Written with great humor and warmth, Elizabeth Berg delivers an endearing story with subtlety and insight.

Published by Ballantine Books.
Available at bookstores everywhere.